ALWAYS
A LADY

Sharon Sala

A KISMET® Romance

METEOR PUBLISHING CORPORATION
Bensalem, Pennsylvania

To ladies everywhere who've had the good luck to find a cowboy and the good sense to keep him.

And to Billy Jack, my cowboy, who's never let me down.

SHARON SALA

Sharon Sala is an Okie and proud of it. She's lived her entire life within seven miles of where she was born. Prague, Oklahoma, where she and her husband farm and ranch, has been her home for the past twenty-seven years. This past year she was nominated by Romantic Times for a Reviewer's Choice Award, and was a RITA finalist in the short contemporary division at the national Romance Writers of America convention. Pretty heady stuff for a farm girl with a head full of daydreams.

Other books by Sharon Sala:

ONE

"My God, Doctor! Can't you fix her face?"

Lily Brownfield stood behind the door of her hospital room and listened, with her heart breaking and tears flowing, as her fiancé, Todd Collins, stood in the hall, berating the plastic surgeon in charge of her case. The bandages had been off less than fifteen minutes, and already her world was falling apart. She heard the disgust in Todd's voice. She didn't want to hear the doctor's response. Yet she stood transfixed as he reluctantly answered her fiancé's frantic question.

"Of course, there will be a time when we can do further surgery to lessen the impact of permanent scarring. But for now, you should be thankful your fiancée is alive and healing. All things worthwhile take time, Mr. Collins. You, as a lawyer, should know that, because nothing grinds slower than the wheels of justice." He smiled gently. "Give her time. Lily is a young, vibrant woman. She needs to heal a bit and then we'll see. Okay?''

"Of course, doctor. Of course," Todd murmured. "But we were going to be married in less than two months. Now it will have to be postponed indefinitely. She certainly won't want to walk down the aisle with a face like . . ." Words failed him. Todd cleared his voice and began again. "I can't have a wife who's . . ." He was almost shouting. "How can she be the perfect wife and hostess now?''

The doctor bit his lip to keep from cursing. In his job, he met all kinds. This perfectly dressed, perfectly educated, perfectly bred man was a perfect jerk. He knew his patient wouldn't agree, but in his estimation, she'd be lucky to be rid of him.

Lily gasped and pressed her fingers tightly against her mouth to keep from crying aloud. She couldn't help it. His words confirmed her worst fears. Lily knew that their relationship was lacking in depth, but everyone always said they'd been the perfect couple. She'd hoped that time and the bonds of matrimony could create the kind of marriage her parents had enjoyed before her mother's untimely death several years earlier.

She squeezed her eyes shut and tried to ignore the fact that her future plans had just come to an abrupt end. Facts were impossible to ignore. She'd seen the look of utter abhorrence on his face when the bandages had come off. Even if she insisted on the marriage taking place, how could she marry someone who cared more about how she was outside than inside? There was only one thing she could do and maintain a sense of control in her life. She'd make the first cut. It wouldn't be easy, but in the long run would save her the most pain.

She opened the door and caught the guilty look on Todd's face before he had time to conceal it.

"Todd," she said quietly, "I think you'd better come inside. It's obvious that we have something to discuss that does not concern my doctor, nor his methods of healing."

The doctor frowned, knowing full well what was about to take place, and wished with all his heart that he could heal more than the bodies of his patients. This beautiful young woman who'd been brought into the emergency room nearly two weeks earlier was going to go home with a long, ugly scar down the side of her face. But in his estimation, it was going to heal faster than the injury her shallow fiancé was about to deal. Sometimes broken hearts were more deadly than the worst of bodily injuries.

Lily stared blindly toward the beach, watching the breakers crashing against the rocks below her house. It had been weeks since she'd been dismissed from the hospital, and still she could not make one simple decision about her future. She didn't see the beauty of the day, nor the gulls swooping toward the sands in raucous abandon. All she kept seeing was an instant replay of Todd's face as she handed him her engagement ring. And his look of guilty relief as he'd stuffed it into his pocket.

He'd tried to hug her.

Why now, Todd? she'd thought. It was much too late. She'd stopped the gesture and pushed away from him. She didn't need his pity, and being held by one of Los Angeles's best young lawyers was suddenly not as appealing as it had been.

"No more pretenses, Todd," she had told him. "You obviously loved my appearance more than you loved me. And I understand that I was not chosen to be a wife as much as a hostess, a pretty foile for your perfect looks, Todd. It seems to me that I still am perfect—the perfect fool."

"But Lily, you don't know . . ."

"I know more than I want to, Todd. I want you to leave. It's going to be up to you to cancel all the arrangements that have been made. You can tell people whatever pretty lie you choose as to why we're no longer being married. I don't have the stomach to pretend."

Her voice shook and she swallowed hard, refusing to break down in front of the man who'd just broken her heart. Lily wanted to scream, she wanted to lash out, but she did neither. It wasn't the ladylike thing to do, and Lily Catherine Brownfield was, above all else, always a lady. Todd had told her it was one of the first things that had attracted him to her. However, it was obviously not enough to maintain a relationship in the face of her injuries.

Todd had stood before her, shamefaced and angry, but he neither refuted her accusations nor handed her back the ring. Instead, he had spun around and walked out of her life.

Lily had closed her eyes, and tears had trickled out from behind her bruised eyelids and down the red gash across her left cheek. But she hadn't wanted to cry. Todd Collins wasn't worth it.

She had walked over to her bed, and fell across the wad of sheets, wondering what she was going to do? There was no way she was going back to work in the same offices and face Todd Collins everyday. Before her accident, she could have worked anywhere. She was a good legal secretary. But she had a sick feeling that kept growing inside her heart that no one would hire someone so disfigured. Todd knew her, was supposed to love her, and he'd been unable to bear the sight of her face. Why would a total stranger feel any differently?

The phone rang, jarring Lily's wayward thoughts back to the present. She blinked, trying to erase the ugly memories of the past. She turned and ran into the house.

"Hello," she answered.

"Lily Kate, where the hell have you been?" Her father's deep, booming voice was a welcome break, even if he did persist in calling her by her childhood nickname.

"I was just outside, Daddy," she said softly. "You know, getting some fresh air and sunshine and all that stuff."

"When are you coming home?" he asked.

He was still furious with her for not letting him punch out Todd Collins. He hadn't liked the ambitious, blond yuppie in the first place. Now he definitely didn't. But his love for his only daughter prevented him from saying I told you so.

Lily sighed. It was more of the same old thing. Every time she stubbed her toe her family wanted her to come home and hide. It was true that this latest event in her life hardly compared to a stubbed toe, but she knew that going home was not going to heal the hurts inside, not this time.

"Daddy, we've discussed this. I love you and I

love my brothers, although having four of them has been, at times, a burden I could have done without." She smiled to herself, knowing that neither she nor her father believed her brothers any kind of burden. "But, under no circumstances am I coming home to hide. You didn't raise me like that."

Morgan Brownfield sighed and ran his fingers through his hair. He'd just had a mouthful of his own preachings thrown back in his face and couldn't argue with his daughter. She had him cold.

"Okay," he muttered. "But if you do decide you want to come home . . . just for a visit mind you . . . you know you don't have to call. Just come."

"I know, Daddy, and thanks. Tell Cole, Buddy, J.D. and Dusty that I said hello. I love you all."

"We love you, too, baby," Morgan answered, and swallowed past a lump in his throat. He could hardly stand the thought of his baby, his only girl, alone and hurting like this. And he still hadn't given up on the thought of punching Todd Collins in the face.

Lily replaced the receiver, sank down onto a hassock and buried her face in her hands. The tears fell. Life was not fair. Her fingers splayed across the groove in her face and unconsciously traced its path from the corner of her eye, down across her cheekbone, almost to the corner of her mouth. It was long, red, and ugly, and Lily wanted to scream at the unjustness of it all.

It hadn't taken long for a drunk driver to change the course of her life. But she knew as she sighed and walked back toward the deck overlooking the ocean that she should be thankful she still had a life. It was just hard to look in the mirror and convince herself of the fact.

A strong gusty breeze caught the heavy fall of her hair, lifting the ash blond curls into the air and playing with the ends before letting them fall in place down her bare back and shoulders. Her matching blue shorts and halter top were cool, comfortable and old. Lily's bare feet were padding across the redwood deck toward a chaise lounge when another breeze gusted across the horizon.

From the corner of her eye, she had a moment's impression of something small and white on the beach below and turned to look. A newspaper was blowing across the sands, leaving sheet after sheet to scatter in the swiftly rising breeze. She frowned. Trash. It was a constant problem.

The beach in front of her house was private, but less than a mile up the sands was a very popular, very public beach. She muttered to herself about the carelessness of strangers as she hurried down her steps to catch the bulk of the paper before it scattered even worse.

The chase was fast and furious as Lily danced about on the sands, trying to outwit the winds that played with the loose pages of newsprint. Finally, puffing and winded, red-faced and sweaty, Lily had captured all but two pages of the paper, which had escaped on the outgoing tide. She started up her deck steps to the garbage can, opened the lid and began stuffing the wadded pages inside when she noticed the paper's origin.

"Good grief," Lily muttered, "*The Daily Oklaho-*

man? How in heaven's name did you get so far from home?''

Curiosity and boredom got the better of her. It might be interesting to see what was happening halfway across the country. She yanked the pages from the garbage can, took them into the house to be straightened and put back into order, to be read later.

She'd piddled at eating an evening meal, snacking from whatever was left in her refrigerator as she browsed through the crumpled paper. It was when she got to the classified section that her interest was piqued.

"Help wanted," Lily mumbled. "Let's see if the job market in Oklahoma is so very different from California."

Nothing caught her attention until she came to a section marked, *General Help*. Four lines in a very generic ad caught her eye and for an instant, her imagination. *Cook wanted - Longren Ranch - Clinton, Oklahoma - 405-555-BULL*.

Lily laughed. She hadn't expected to, and she realized she hadn't in a very long time. Just the sound surprised her. Tears came to her eyes as she tried to remember the last time she'd even wanted to laugh.

"555-Bull," she grinned. "Who do they think they're kidding?"

She looked at the date on the top of the page and noticed with surprise that the paper was less than three days old. She wondered if the job had been filled, then wondered if she'd lost her mind. Why should she care whether the job of ranch cook was still open? She'd gone through four years of college, worked long and hard at Prentiss and Sons as a beginning secretary, and then private, legal secretary. She didn't need to worry about a cook's job.

That's what she kept telling herself all the way to the telephone. A long decorative mirror hanging over her sofa threw back a reflection that made her frown. The scar on her face was vivid. Her exertion earlier in the day while chasing the blowing paper had aggravated the new, healing tissue. Who would want to look at a face like that?

Her stomach churned as she sat down, grabbed the phone, and dialed the number. On the sixth ring, a man's deep, sleepy voice answered and Lily instantly remembered, although too late, that there was a two hour time difference. *Lord!* she thought. *He'll think I'm crazy.*

"This better be good," the man's deep drawl warned, "because it's too damn late for phone calls."

Silence answered him.

"Whoever's on the other end better start talking. It's your nickel and I'm too tired to play games."

Lily took a deep breath and blurted out. "Is this Mr. Longren in Oklahoma?"

"Yeah," came the sleepy response. "What can I do for you?"

"Is the cook's job still open?" Lily asked.

Silence answered her, and then a husky chuckle sent shivers up her spine as his voice softened and the anger seemed to disappear.

"You called me at a quarter to eleven at night to ask about a job?" The laughter was still evident in his voice, but the question was sincere.

"Yes . . ." Lily stuttered, suddenly put on the

defensive about committing herself. "I just wondered if it was still open."

"Hell, yes, honey," he said. "Are you interested?"

Lily gritted her teeth. Honey!

"What does it pay?" she asked.

"Can you cook?" he fired back.

"Yes, I can cook. I wouldn't be asking otherwise," Lily said sharply.

The amount he named made her stop and take a second look at the ad.

"You mean you're paying that much just for a cook? Who in God's name are you feeding?"

Case sat up in bed, wiped his hand across his face, and smiled to himself. He liked the spunky sound of her voice.

"More than a dozen men who're helping with spring roundup. It's three meals a day, six days a week, and a place to sleep. Take it or leave it." And then before he forgot, he added, "The job is only temporary. Three months and then the extra help I've hired is gone. I don't keep a cook year-round. Most of my regular help is married. They have their own cooks."

Lily was silent, her mind racing as she absorbed the implications of disappearing for three months to get her head and life back in order. The thought was intriguing.

"Well," the man drawled, "are you interested?"

"When do I start?" Lily couldn't believe she'd just said that.

"When can you get here?" he fired back.

"Give me two days to get my life in order and my plane tickets, and the directions to your ranch. You just hired yourself a cook."

"Good," he said. "Just hurry. If the men have to eat much more of Pete's cooking, they're going to leave. But never mind about directions. When you get a flight number, call back. I'll have someone pick you up in Oklahoma City."

"Right," she answered, and then hung up the phone with shaky hands. She didn't know whether to laugh or cry. What in heaven's name had she just done?

The Oklahoma airport was unfamiliar. And, like all airports, her plane had landed at one end of the building, and her luggage was to be retrieved at the other on a different level. It figured.

She'd just pulled the last bag from the conveyor when she heard her name being paged. Bags in tow behind her on a wheeled luggage carrier, she started in search of the Information Booth where she'd been ordered to appear. She didn't know who or what to expect. Neither she nor Mr. Longren had had the foresight to give each other any identifying characteristics. Lily's reason was painfully obvious as she ignored the curious glances of the people she passed. How would she have worded it? Just look for the blonde with her face in pieces? The best she could hope for was to look for someone wearing a cowboy hat. Surely that would help. The people lived and worked on a ranch, they must look like cowboys. It was a bad idea. She changed her tactics and searched the area for someone who seemed to be waiting. Once again, nearly everyone she saw fit that description.

"You wouldn't be the cook?"

The voice behind her sent her spinning around.

She looked down into the wizened face of the tiniest man she'd ever seen. He couldn't have been much over five feet tall, but he was wearing a tall hat and boots to match that added several inches to his diminutive size.

"Excuse me?" Lily asked, trying not to stare at the maze of wrinkles running down his face. It reminded her of her own mark, and she unconsciously touched her cheek with her fingers.

"I said, you wouldn't by any chance be the cook for Longren Ranch, would you? I don't suppose we'd be this lucky." The grin that accompanied his remark made Lily smile in return.

"Are you Mr. Longren?"

"Shoot no, miss," he cackled. "Name's Arloe, Arloe Duffy, but you can call me Duff. Everyone else does. I guess that means you're Miss Brownfield."

"Call me Lily," she said, and watched the little man's face for a sign that would indicate he was shocked or disgusted by her slow-healing injuries. There was none.

"Lily it is," he crowed. "Boy howdy, the guys are gonna eat crow tonight when they get a look at you. They been expectin' some old lady on her last pegs."

"Why in the world would they think that?" Lily asked.

"Who else would want to come bury herself in a kitchen for the better part of three months except someone who ain't got anything better to do?"

Duff realized the moment he'd spoken that he might have just put his entire booted foot in his mouth. He blushed, started to stammer and then yanked his hat off his head. Fuzzy tufts of grey hair sprang up in wild abandon. He smashed his hat against his chest in abject apology.

"Shoot, Miss Lily. Don't mind me. I ain't seen anyone as young and purty as you in a month of Sundays. It just clabbered my brain. You know what I mean, and alls I can say is we're real proud to have you at the Bar L. Especially if you can cook better than Pete."

Hearing Duff say that she was young and pretty went a long way toward soothing the ache in her heart, even if she didn't quite believe he meant it.

"Well," she answered, "I don't know about Pete's cooking. But I have a father and four older brothers who can certainly vouch for mine. I *can* cook just about anything, and lots of it."

"Ooooee," Duff crowed. "I can hardly wait. Come on Miss Lily, let's get crackin'." He shoved the crumpled hat back on his head, grabbed her luggage, and motioned for her to follow. They headed down a long hallway.

"Call me Lily," she reminded him, but he was too far ahead of her to hear. She hitched at the waistband of her pink linen slacks, smoothed the short matching jacket down to her slender waist, and followed the little man as fast as she could.

"Here it is," Duff announced, as he turned into another set of gates, the sixth since leaving the main highway, and pointed toward a white, two-story house and a multitude of outbuildings.

"It looks like the house on that television show, *Dallas,*" Lily replied.

"What? You mean Southfork? That's just across

the border into Texas. I seen it a couple of times myself.''

Lily's mouth dropped. "You mean it really exists?"

"Sure," Duff answered. "Different folks own it now, and call it by a different name, but it's still the same place. Look," Duff pointed, "there's the boss now."

Lily stared. She couldn't make out one man from the other. All she could see were cows milling, calves bawling, men running, and dust . . . everywhere.

She got out of the blue pickup truck, dusted off her pink slacks and jacket, and adjusted her sunglasses. She smoothed the honey-colored fall of her hair slightly across her left cheek to hide as much as possible of her scarred face and tried not to wrinkle her nose at the pungent aroma of fresh manure and dust that assailed her.

"How can I tell which one is . . . ?"

Her words froze in the back of her throat as one tall, dusty man separated himself from the melee and turned to face them. His stance was instantly still and out of place in the constantly moving scene before her. Something about his demeanor made her think of ancient kings and royalty. It had to do with the way he ignored the chaos around him and the way he cocked his head back as he looked their way.

Lily's heart jumped, and she resisted the urge to turn and run. Even from this distance she could tell he was big . . . very big . . . and he was coming their way.

Case Longren was hot, dirty, and sick to death

of the smell of dust and blood. They'd been cutting young bulls all morning, deftly removing their ability to sire young with one swift stroke of the knife and thereby turning them into steers that would eventually find their way to someone's dinner table.

He'd almost forgotten that today was the day his new cook was to arrive. In fact, he had forgotten it until he'd seen Duff's blue pickup truck turning into the yard. He watched out of the corner of his eye for a glimpse of his new hired hand. It was the first time he'd ever done anything as foolish as hire someone, sight unseen, no references asked, over a phone. He absently wondered if he'd just bought the proverbial "pig in a poke."

His wandering thoughts slammed into his gut with rude force as the pickup door opened and a young, blond woman emerged, towering over little Duff by nearly a foot.

"Sweet bird of youth," he muttered, and tossed the end of his rope to one of the men nearby. She wasn't a pig, that much was evident, but she was damn sure pink . . . and as out of place as a heifer in a pen full of steers. "Here, Harris. Help the boys finish up here. I'll be back later."

Something was different about this lady. He could tell that even from a distance. Case knew women, and this one didn't fidget or preen. She stood stock-still, letting the dust and wind carry whatever came her way without shading her face or brushing at her clothing. In fact, the closer he came, the more he imagined that she was holding her breath. He scoffed at himself as being fanciful and started worrying about what he was going to do with her. Surely to

God she wasn't actually a cook by trade. He could tell by the cut of her clothes and hairstyle that money played a part in her life.

"Miss Brownfield?" he asked, hoping that he'd been wrong about her identity.

Maybe the cook was coming on the next flight. But his hopes were dashed when she nodded her head slightly and held out her hand. If she'd just handed him a snake, he wouldn't have been more surprised. There was no way he could shake her hand. She had no idea what all he'd been doing with it all morning.

"I'm sorry," he said, and pointed back at the men and cattle, hoping that she'd understand without going into details, "I'm too dirty to shake hands with you, miss."

"I'll wash, Mr. Longren," Lily said quietly, and grasped his hand and shook it before he had time to object.

Lightning!

Case blinked and looked up, expecting to see thunderheads boiling overhead. No clouds, no nothing but the ever-present sun burning down on top of them. He stared blankly at the slender hand still grasping his huge, dirty one, then back up at her face, hidden by sunglasses and that glorious mane of hair, and dropped it as if he'd just been burned.

"Miss Brownfield, you'll have to pardon my asking, but surely cooking is not your chosen profession?"

Lily looked into his dust-covered face, the three-day growth of thick, black stubble shaded by a wide-brimmed, black Stetson, also covered in a thin, persistent layer of dust, and saw blue so clear that she felt she was staring into pieces of the sky behind him.

She stifled the gasp that shot up her throat and knew that those piercing sky-blue eyes would see everything. Instantly, she turned her face slightly, unwilling just yet to see the look of shock she knew would come when he saw her face.

"No," she finally answered, staring at a spot just over his shoulder, "but I can cook, and you said I could come. Does this mean you're sending me away without even a trial period?"

The pain in her voice was evident, yet her demeanor betrayed none of the fear she was experiencing.

"Hell, no!" he said sharply. "My word is good. I'm just surprised, that's all."

He turned to Duff, who was standing to one side and grinning from ear to ear.

Arloe Duffy knew just how the boss felt. The lady had knocked him sideways, too. She was a real looker. And that little ol' scratch on her face didn't amount to much.

"Take her stuff to the house, Duff. I'll walk up with Miss Brownfield. We'll talk on the way."

"Yessirree," Duff crowed, hopped back into his pickup truck and headed for the house. He could almost taste supper.

"Please call me Lily," she asked, as they started toward the house.

"Okay. Lily it is. The same goes for me. The men call me Case, or Boss, whatever's comfortable."

She nodded and quickened her stride, trying to

keep up with the distance his long legs covered in a step.

"So, Lily Brownfield," Case asked, as they entered the house. "Where do you live, when you're not here, that is?" He smiled softly, trying to hide his growing curiosity with innocent questions.

"L.A.," she answered.

Once more Case was dumbstruck. He leaned against the kitchen counter and shoved his hat to the back of his head.

Lily noted by the band of clean skin that appeared that his skin was a very dark shade of nut brown beneath the dust. A vague curiosity slid through her thoughts before she had time to squelch it. *I wonder if he's that brown all over?* She blushed and then frowned at herself.

"California?" he finally was able to mutter, wondering what the frown was for.

She nodded and sighed, running her shaky fingers through her hair and adjusting her sunglasses across her nose. Here it comes.

"What in hell would make someone as young and pretty as you come halfway across the country to cook for a bunch of filthy cowhands for three months? Surely you don't imagine that this is going to be a romantic lark?"

Lily spun around, yanked her sunglasses off her nose, and swept the hair away from her face in one angry gesture.

"Do I look like I'm looking for romance, Mr. Longren?"

Case grunted as if he'd just been kicked in the solar plexus. God in heaven, what had happened to her? He knew now was not the time to ask.

Lily waited, expecting to see horror darken the blue of his gaze, or watch him turn away in disgust as the full measure of her injury was revealed. But to her surprise, he did neither. He stood, watching her anger, yet not responding to it by word or action.

"Well?" Lily finally asked, her chin thrust upwards in defense, waiting for the thrust of his judgement.

"Well what?" he finally remarked.

"Do I stay?"

"Hell, yes," Case grumbled. "I already told you that. Just don't think you can make a bunch of Oklahoma cowboys eat alfalfa sprouts and sunflower seeds. Out here we eat beef, and feed the green stuff to the cattle."

Lily smiled. It was obvious that he wanted her to stay. It felt as if a huge weight had just disappeared from her shoulders.

"Yes, Boss," she said sharply. "Now would you please show me where I'll be sleeping, and where the kitchen and foodstuffs are?"

Lily knew she'd just been rude again and regretted her sharp manner the moment she'd spoken. It was too late to take back what she'd said, so she tried softening her words with a smile.

Case stared, dumbfounded by her beauty as her lips curved upwards. He no longer even noticed the red gash running the length of her cheek. He was too lost in wondering what it would taste like to kiss that smile.

"What did you say?" he finally asked.

"I said, where do you expect me to sleep?"

In my bed, came instantly to mind, and then Case

wisely kept the thought to himself. He decided to stick to the facts.

"Come on," he muttered, "I'll show you to your room and then fill you in on the whereabouts of kitchen supplies and mealtimes. The rest is up to you."

TWO

They were coming. Lily could hear their easy laughter and tired jokes as they came up the back steps of the house. Her heart skipped a beat and then made up for it by beating double time as the first of the men entered the room.

Two long tables had been temporarily set up in the huge kitchen and adjoining dining area with an odd assortment of folding chairs shoved in place. There was plenty of room for the promised number of men that would be expecting food three times a day, six days a week. Lily prayed that she hadn't been off in calculating the correct quantities of food to prepare. She'd mentally counted what she used to fix for her father and four brothers and then multiplied it by six. If the men ate more than that, they were pigs.

Lily didn't know how the food had been served by her predecessor, Pete, but she knew from experience that the easiest way to feed a crowd was buffet style. She had the food set out in steaming array on the long, island work counter with the desserts and drinks on a roomy sideboard against a wall in the dining room.

Silence reigned as the last man squeezed himself into the kitchen and stood mashed against the wall, trying to get a glimpse of the new lady cook that they'd all been talking about. One cowboy couldn't see her, but it was his short, succinct comment that broke the silence and . . . for Lily . . . the ice.

"Well," he drawled, "I can't see you, lady, but I can damn sure smell the food. If you smell as purty as it does, you'll be all right."

Everyone laughed as Lily blushed. She had dreaded facing them, knowing that she'd see the shock and then disgust on their faces as she turned her scar their direction. But she was wrong. Very few were even looking at anything but the food, and the ones that eyed her seemed to be flirting, not frowning. Lily was amazed. Was it possible that she'd built up an over-exaggeration of how she looked in her own mind? She'd have to wait and see. For the time being, cooking had taken her mind off all her troubles. It felt good to be this tired again.

Another man spoke up and from what he said, Lily quickly determined that this was the much maligned Pete.

"I don't even care if it tastes bad," Pete drawled. "I've never been so glad to get rid of a job in my life. I was getting dishpan hands."

This time the laughter was an uproar and even Lily could not contain her mirth. It lightened the mood immediately.

"The food is ready and it's buffet style," Lily

said. "Does someone give the blessing before you eat, or . . ."

"Not usually," Case answered.

Lily jumped. She hadn't known Case was behind her. She turned and stared. She hardly recognized him. He'd shaved! And the face that stared back at her sent her heart into overtime.

What a stubborn chin and jaw had been hiding beneath that three-day growth of beard! And who would have suspected such clean, strong lines existed beneath the dust he'd been wearing earlier? Case Longren wasn't just good-looking. He was handsome. Lily suspected he knew it. He was smiling at her with something akin to teasing.

She turned away from his stare and tried to ignore the fact that he was right behind her. But he *was* the boss. She supposed he could stand anywhere he chose.

"However, that doesn't mean it's not a good thing to start," he continued. "I'll do the honors tonight; tomorrow will be someone else's turn. Okay, men?"

Lily shivered. She wondered how long he'd been watching her. The thought was unnerving. Agreeable murmurs took away any embarrassment Lily might have felt for speaking out of turn about saying a prayer before the meal. It was such a normal part of her life that she'd forgotten many people did not practice the habit.

She bowed her head and gripped the counter with shaky fingers, thanking God for the fact that she'd survived the first day of this crazy idea without falling on her face.

"Amen," Case finally said, and many of the men echoed his word.

Lily blinked and raised her head. She'd been so nervous she hadn't heard a word he'd said. She had to get herself under control. It wasn't like her to be disorganized. She smoothed her hand down the side of her denim wraparound skirt and tucked her blue-striped blouse neatly back into the waistband. If she looked calm, maybe she'd feel calm.

"My gosh," one of the men muttered, "I may actually survive these three months after all. Real food!"

Lily surveyed the overflowing table as the men grabbed plates and made two lines on either side of the buffet, teasing and laughing as they heaped on the food. She'd done it! A little feeling of accomplishment crept into her heart. It was the first good feeling she could remember in a long, long time.

Case knew that if he was any kind of man, he should be apologizing to Lily Brownfield with hat in hand, but he was too hungry to take the time. Alfalfa sprouts and sunflower seeds indeed! The table looked great! Somehow she'd taken the same type of food that Pete had managed to boil to death or aptly burn and turned it into appetizing food.

He scooped hungrily into a long pan of lasagna, and took heaping helpings of two kinds of cold salads and a couple of fried chicken legs. He lingered over the hot biscuits, slathering butter on two before being jostled by the men behind him as they urged him to hurry. As he entered the dining room, he eyed the pans of apple crisp on the sideboard and stopped to scoop up a heaping dish of dessert before he dared go sit down. If he waited until he was ready for dessert, he was afraid that it would be gone. He'd never seen the men so eager for a meal.

The first bite was better than expected. He chewed, resisting the urge to moan in pleasure and then looked up in surprise as he saw Lily watching him for a reaction. He smiled as best he could around the mouthful and then winked his approval. The look on her face was worth it. She looked like she'd just swallowed a toad as she turned and fled into the kitchen.

Case grinned to himself and attacked the rest of his food with relish. He hadn't hired a pig in a poke after all. In fact, he'd hired a very capable, and from the quick glimpses she would allow of herself, a very pretty cook.

The last man was finally leaving the kitchen. Lily thought she was going to have to beg him not to scrape the bowls.

"There'll be more tomorrow," Lily had teased softly. "I'm not going anywhere."

The blush that had crept up his neck matched the one on her face as he looked up and finally focused on her cheek.

She watched his eyebrows raise, his mouth go slack with shock, and his eyes follow the path from the corner of her eye, down her cheek, toward her mouth. He swallowed, turned away and then back again, staring intently at her scar. But the remark he made was not what Lily had expected.

He licked a bit of remaining apple crisp from his fingers, looked back at her cheek and drawled, "If you fight as good as you cook, lady, I'd hate to see what the other guy looked like."

Lily's mouth dropped. The man sauntered out of

the back door and into the fading daylight as Lily sank limply onto a kitchen stool.

Suddenly the stress of the day set in as Lily began to shake. She surveyed the mountain of dirty pans and dishes still to clean and buried her face in her hands. *Dear Lord, I'm tired.*

Before she had time to bemoan her fate, she felt a tug at the back of her head. She looked up. Case was yanking lightly at the thick braid hanging down the middle of her back.

"Are you all right?" he asked, eyeing the pallor of her face.

The protective feeling that had swept over him when he'd walked into the kitchen and seen her sitting with her head bowed in despair had hit all the way down to the pit of his stomach. It surprised him. He couldn't remember the last time he'd worried about a woman in this manner.

"I'm fine," Lily answered shortly as she ducked her head, pulled her braid out of his teasing fingers, and darted toward the table to gather up the dirty dishes.

Case stood watching her work, knowing that his presence was making her uncomfortable. He'd give a week's pay to know what had happened to Lily Brownfield, but tonight was obviously not the time to ask.

"Breakfast is at six," he said shortly before turning and disappearing into the living area of his home.

"Yes, Boss," Lily answered sharply. But her words were unnecessary. Case Longren was gone.

The next few days passed in a blur of heat, smells of cooking food, hungry men, and aching back and feet, but Lily survived. And, each day it became a little easier.

On this day, she had at least an hour before she needed to start the noon meal. She walked out onto the back porch with a tall glass of iced tea and slid sideways onto the porch swing, putting her feet on the opposite arm rest. It felt good to sit down with her feet up. Her navy blue culottes and matching blouse were cool and comfortable and still practical for her job.

She leaned back, letting the roomy legs of her divided skirt slide upward just the tiniest bit and closed her eyes as she ran the cold glass of tea along her forehead and then down the side of her face, relishing the drip of condensation. She sighed, raised the glass to her lips, and took a long, deep drink of the slightly sweet liquid. Tea had never tasted so good.

"Ooowee, honey, but you sure look fine."

The voice was unexpected and unfamiliar and Lily almost fell out of the porch swing as she scrambled to get to her feet and smooth down her skirt. She turned her face away, shielding the side with the scar from prying eyes.

She recognized the man's face, knew the men called him Lane, but she didn't know whether it was a first or last name.

"Was there something you needed?" Lily asked sharply. She didn't like his familiar manner or the way his look lingered too long for decency on her breasts and legs.

"Always," he drawled.

Lily blushed furiously. She didn't like this man at all.

"Then why are you here? Did Case send you up to the house for something?"

The mention of the boss's name made Lane turn around and sneak a quick look toward the arena where all the aspects of roundup were still in progress.

"Naw," he answered. "I just wanted to take the time to tell you in person that I think you're a fine-looking woman and a great cook to boot."

"Thank you," Lily answered and started back in the house. "I have to go inside now." She wanted this meeting brought to an end. There was something ugly about the way he kept searching her body. And then his next words confirmed her suspicions and made her even more certain that this was a man from whom to steer clear.

"Is that scar on your face the only one? Mind you, it's hardly noticeable. Especially on a woman built as fine as you, honey."

"I don't think it's any of your damned business," Lily shouted, and slammed the door behind her.

She couldn't believe she'd just done that. She'd lost her temper and composure in a heartbeat. It wasn't like her to be so unladylike. She was still shaking from shock and anger when Case stormed into the kitchen.

"What the hell did Lane Turney want up here?"

Case had been on his way to the house to make a phone call when he'd seen his hired hand leaving the yard and Lily making a hasty exit from the porch into the house. The streak of anger that had swept over him at the sight of her consorting with one of his men spurred his angry question.

Lily spun around, fury in her every gesture at the

manner in which he'd asked. He acted as if she'd invited the man to linger about and shirk his work.

"For starters," Lily said quietly, anger turning the green in her eyes to a dark jade, "he wanted to know if I had scars anywhere else on my body besides my face."

Case sucked in his breath. The hurt in her voice tugged at his heart and conscience. It was not what he'd expected her to say, and he wished that he had counted to ten before he'd opened his mouth. He knew how he'd sounded, and he knew he was wrong. But it was too late to take back what had already been said. Before he could apologize, Lily stunned him as she continued.

"I'll tell you, like I told him. It's nobody's damned business. I cook. I don't fraternize. I don't want to. I hope I've made myself abundantly clear."

Case watched her gathering her wits about her like a queen. She straightened to full height, tilted her head back until the scarred portion of her face was in plain sight, and dared him to make another remark.

"I'm sorry, Lily," Case said quietly. "And I can promise that won't happen again. I'll talk to the man myself."

He walked out of the door with purpose in his step and left Lily standing in the middle of the kitchen. He was going to tear a strip off of Lane Turney. And then he thought, *who's going to tear a strip off of me?* He deserved it and he knew it. Case wouldn't admit, even to himself, that the feeling he'd experienced was jealousy, not concern that his hired hand was shirking his assigned work.

Lily watched the door slam shut and turned away from the gust of wind that came with it. The wind was hot, an echo of her emotions. She tried to take a deep, calming breath, but when it came out, it sounded more like a sob. A strand of hair fell across her eyes, and she lifted her hand up to tuck in back in place. As she did, her fingers grazed across the tender area on her cheek, down the slow-healing gash. She began to shake. The kitchen walls began to close in on her. The hallway leading toward her bedroom beckoned. Solitude! It was just what she needed.

Tears welled. She squeezed her eyes shut, fiercely trying to block out the pain of Lane's question and Case's angry accusation. It didn't work. For the first time since her accident and her fiancé's betrayal, she wished she'd just gone home and let her father and brothers take care of her world. Right now, she didn't think she was able to do it herself.

She staggered down the hallway to her room and fell onto the bed. The inviting homespun decor did not soothe her spirit, nor give her any feelings of comfort. It was nothing more than a place to hide. She buried her face in the curve of one arm, clutched the coverlet with her fingers and let out the pain.

It was then she cried. At first there were tears, silent, swift, and sudden. But then came the sobs that deepened into gut-wrenching painful gasps for air.

She cried for the unjustness of life that had changed her world from happy and safe into life-threatening and pain. She cried for the loss of a love that had obviously never been true. She cried for the comfort of her family's arms that were too far away to help. And she cried because if Todd had been the man she'd imagined, today would have been her wedding day.

And then she was lifted from her bed, gathered against a wall of muscle, a fiercely beating heart and strong arms and gentle hands that held her tight and kept her from flying apart.

Lily was too far gone to realize she was being held and, when she did, too distraught to care. All she could concentrate on was the comfort she was receiving and the knowledge that for a moment, someone made the hurt lessen.

The sound of her crying had pulled him down the hall. And when he'd stepped into her room, it had pulled him apart, a piece at a time. The heart-rending sound of her pain was overwhelming. He'd never been so helpless and so furious all at the same time, knowing that he was partially to blame. Dear God, but he wanted to take away her hurt. He wrapped his arms around her trembling body and cradled her gently, whispering softly against her ear as he bore the brunt of her weight against his chest.

Damn but she's soft! And there isn't a curve out of place on this lady. She feels just about perfect in my arms.

His wandering thoughts startled him. He had no business letting his imagination run riot like this. It didn't seem right to be enjoying this when she was so unhappy.

"Stop," Case begged, as he held Lily's shaking body in his arms. "Please, Lily. Stop crying. You're going to make yourself sick. I'm sorry. I swear to God I'm sorry. I didn't mean to hurt your feelings, and as for Lane, it'll never happen again."

The quiet strength of his voice soaked and soothed

her hysteria. Her sobs lessened, her shaking quieted, and the tears fell slower until they finally ceased to exist. The arms holding her loosened gently, and Lily felt her face tilted upward. She opened her eyes into a blaze of blue and tried to turn away, suddenly reminded of the view Case Longren had of her.

"Don't turn away from me, Lily," he whispered. He cupped her face in his hands, caressing the tender curve of her cheeks with rough, callused palms as he wiped away the last of her tears with his thumbs. "Talk to me about this."

The soft, gentle manner in which he traced her face lessened the embarrassment Lily felt as he touched her so intimately.

But then she shrugged out of his arms, shocked at the way she'd clung to him only moments before. She turned away in confusion.

Case watched her wrap her arms around herself and knew that she was gathering strength to continue. She was some lady, his cook.

"There's nothing much to talk about," Lily finally answered. She turned to face him and stuffed her hands in her pockets to hide their tremble. "I went to a bridal shower. I started home and a drunk driver changed the shape of my face . . . and my life . . . forever. Is that what you wanted to hear?"

Her words were angry and defensive. Case ached for her.

"Is that why you wanted this job? Because your life took such a drastic change? Or are you hiding from your life by coming halfway across the country to take a job you're obviously overqualified for."

"This job, as you call it, is little more than what I did for the last twelve years of my life before I finally moved away from home. My mother died when I was thirteen. I became chief cook and bottle washer for my father and four older brothers. They all had jobs and I didn't. Feeding them became my job. In the beginning, I wasn't very good at it, but I got better. Daddy let me falter and helped me along the way. My brothers never complained about my failures. It took me several years to realize that they'd given me that job to help me get through the emptiness I felt when my mother died."

"Is that where you were living when you had your accident?" Case asked.

Lily hesitated. Now it got sticky, and she wasn't certain how much of her private life she felt like revealing.

"No, I was living in L.A., remember? I grew up outside of Laguna Beach."

Case felt her reticence. There was more; he could tell.

"So what did you do in L.A.? Surely you weren't a cook?"

"I worked as a legal secretary in a law firm."

Case watched the pain growing as her lips tightened and the fury in her eyes turned them back to that darker shade of jade he'd noticed was a signal of her anger.

"And . . ." he coaxed.

"And I had my accident, and I left to come out here," she answered.

It was too pat and too quick.

"And there was no one in L.A. who tried to stop you? Surely you had friends, Lily. Couldn't you go back to your old job?"

Anger exploded, surprising Lily as much as it did Case.

"My fiancé wanted his ring back because he didn't want to walk down the aisle with a bride who had a face like this. I couldn't go back and work in the same office with a man who hated the sight of me, now could I?"

Case grabbed her hand as she gestured angrily toward her face. His eyes narrowed until they were mere slits of blue.

"Are you telling me that a man who claimed to love you wouldn't marry you because of that little scratch on your face?"

Little scratch!

She caught her breath and blinked back a fresh set of tears. She'd be damned if she cried in front of this man again.

"Well, Lily Brownfield, if you ask me, which you didn't, I'll tell you one damned thing is obvious as hell. You're the luckiest woman alive that the bastard dumped you because he doesn't deserve the ground you walk on."

Lily stared. She couldn't help herself. Case was furious, and if man could have breathed fire, she'd have sworn she saw smoke pouring from his nostrils.

"Well," she muttered in shock and embarrassment. "Thank you . . . I think."

"You're damned well welcome," Case snarled. "Are you going to be all right?"

"I think I'll probably be just fine. All in all, I think I'd rather be feeding your crew today than having a wedding anyway."

Case's silence was deafening.

"Today was to have been your wedding day?" he asked quietly.

Lily nodded, afraid that speaking would call back the pain.

"If you'll excuse me," Lily finally said, walking quickly past him. "I've got to get busy or dinner will be raw. But the way the men eat, I doubt they'd notice."

She was nearly running by the time she got to the kitchen. Case walked out right behind her and through the kitchen door before she had time to take another breath. She watched the stiff thrust of his shoulder as he pushed his way through the opening and shuddered as he slammed the door so hard behind him that the glass rattled in its frame.

She heard him start a litany of curses that lingered in her head and heart long after she'd lost sight and sound of her boss. It did her soul a tiny bit of good to think that someone besides herself damned the ground Todd Collins walked on.

A couple of hours later, the men entered in their usual boisterous fashion and Lily's attention was claimed by the hustle and bustle of feeding the starving crew. Case was in and out so quickly Lily wouldn't have even noticed were it not for the fact that he asked for some aluminum foil with which to wrap his food.

"I want to take this with me or I'll have to skip the meal altogether," Case said. "Fix one for Duff, too. We need to go check on a herd of cattle on the back forty and see if we missed any weaning calves. I don't want to have to repeat this job at a later date."

Lily wouldn't look him in the eye. She quickly

prepared the sandwiches and wished she'd kept her mouth shut. At least when no one had known, they hadn't had to feel sorry for her.

"Lily," he ordered softly so that none of the other men could hear, "don't ever turn your face away from anyone again. Do you hear me?"

Lily glared. He had no right.

Case glared back. He didn't know what it was going to take, but before she left, he'd see a smile in her eyes as well as on that sexy mouth, or he'd die trying.

"Oh," he said as he started out the door, "tomorrow is Saturday. After breakfast, just leave the fixings for sandwiches or the like. Make up a list of what you'll need for the coming week, and I'll have someone take you into Clinton to shop. Buy what you need. I trust your judgment. I have an open account at the supermarket. Just tell them you work for Longren. They'll know what to do."

Lily nodded and watched him disappear with the sandwiches. In spite of the remaining men and the constant noise, the room felt empty. Lily bit her bottom lip and turned away from the window. She wouldn't stand like some love-starved pup and watch him walk away. She had no intention of ever putting her faith and trust in a man again, no matter how kind he pretended to be.

Just after breakfast Lane Turney appeared at the back door with his hat in hand and a soulful expression on his face.

"Miss Lily," he said, looking everywhere but at her, "I'm to take you to town to do the shopping just as soon as you're ready."

Lane held his breath, hoping that she wouldn't challenge him and refuse to go. He'd overheard Case's orders yesterday and wanted this chance to make time with the fancy cook. He'd been mad as hell yesterday when the boss had jumped all over him for coming to the house. Where did the boss get off telling him what woman he could and couldn't see? And Lane didn't care if she did have a gash down the side of her face. Her beauty almost made up for it, and her body damned sure did. He'd heard Case tell Duff to take her to town within the hour. If his luck held, they'd be gone before Duff ever made it to the main house.

Lily was confused. She knew that Case had been very angry with the way Lane had talked to her yesterday. She couldn't imagine his expecting her to ride all the way into town with a man who'd insulted her. She stared long and hard at Lane, watching his downcast manner and refusal to meet her eyes and decided that Case must have given him quite a downdressing.

Lane realized that he'd better do some fast talking or he wouldn't get to first base with this one. He shuffled his feet childishly and mumbled, "I'm real sorry about yesterday, miss. I didn't mean nothin' by what I said. I'm not too good with words, but I meant to pay you a compliment, not hurt your feelings."

When she didn't speak, he ventured a quick glance up and caught a quiet, watchful expression on her face.

"I'm not going to say I've forgotten what you said, Lane. I just want you to keep your distance from me. Is that understood?"

"Yes, ma'am. Are you ready?"

"Yes." Lily sighed. She wished with all her heart that Case hadn't done this, but she didn't know how to refuse without causing a big fuss that would simply call attention to the incident all over again. "Just let me get my purse and my list."

Lane watched the gentle sway of her hips beneath her red slacks as she walked away, and when she came back with her belongings, he snuck a quick look at the thrust of her ample breasts against the matching sleeveless blouse. They walked silently to the station wagon. Lane quickly ran to open the door to the passenger side and stood back for Lily to be seated.

She rolled her eyes heavenward, prayed for this day to be over soon, and stared out the window as Lane slid under the steering wheel.

"We're on our way," he said cheerily.

Lily's refusal to answer him didn't dampen his spirits one bit. He had her to himself all the way to town, as well as all the way back. There was plenty of time to soften her up.

The only problem with Lane's plan was that Lily wasn't in on it. She hadn't volunteered one remark the entire trip. She finally answered his questions with single syllable responses and managed to infuriate him to the point of explosion.

"We're here," he snapped, as he pulled into the parking lot of a huge supermarket. "How much time do you need?" he asked. "I'll pick you up when you say."

Lily looked down at her watch, scanned the list in her hand, and answered.

"Give me a couple of hours." Lily slipped out of

the car and quickly shut the door, anxious to get away from the constant barrage of sly looks and innuendos that she'd had to endure all the way to Clinton.

"I'll give you more than that, miss high and mighty," Lane muttered, as he drove out of the parking lot and headed for a local bar. He needed fortification and nerve for what he'd planned, and Lane always found that in a bottle.

"Boss," Duff said, as he walked back into the barn scratching his head. "Miss Lily's already gone. One of the men said he saw her leaving in the station wagon nearly a half hour ago."

Case looked up from the calf he'd been doctoring and frowned. "Was she by herself?"

"Nope," Duff answered. "Someone was driving, but they couldn't tell who it was."

Case shrugged. He didn't think much of it, but all the same it puzzled him. Who would take it upon himself to chauffeur Lily into town and chance angering him by shirking assigned work? The answer was almost on his lips as Case straightened up and started to look around, checking to see who was not at their duties, when one of the men ran into the barn shouting at the top of his voice.

"Boss, that damned herd bull is out again and madder than hell. I guess he thinks we're stealing all his girlfriends."

Case dropped everything and motioned for all the men to come on the run. The bull was big and the least trustworthy of any animal he'd ever owned. Every year he made himself a promise that he'd sell the cantankerous animal and buy another one with a better nature. It wasn't safe to have such an animal on the place. But every year the calves he got from the sire were such fine ones that he kept giving the dangerous animal another chance.

"Get the hot shot," Case yelled at Duff.

They rounded the barn and saw the angry animal, head down, pawing huge clouds of dust in the air with his forefeet as he bluffed and bellowed his way toward the pen where the cows and calves were being separated.

Duff went after the portable electric prod as several other men loosened their lariats. It took almost an hour before the bull was under control and back in his pen. By that time, Case had forgotten to check and see who had taken Lily to town.

Lily sat on a stack of fifty pound sacks of dog food and looked out the supermarket windows, watching for Lane and the ranch station wagon. She'd been waiting for nearly thirty minutes past the promised time. Finally, she saw the wagon pulling into the lot. She frowned as Lane swerved sharply, narrowly missing a woman and child pushing their cart across the lot. She looked around for the bag boy, motioning to show him that her ride had finally arrived.

It took Lily and three boys to push all the carts full of food she'd purchased. She'd estimated enough to last the week. They had them outside and ready to unload when Lane finally pulled up in the loading lane.

"Hey, pretty lady," he called loudly, as he stepped out of the station wagon and staggered toward her. "Load her up. We got places to go before I take you back to the salt mines."

Lily gasped and felt bile rising in her throat. He was drunk! Just the thought made her panic. A drunk had nearly ended her life. There was no way on earth she was getting into the car with him as driver. She motioned for the bag boys to wait.

"Lane, let me drive. You've been drinking."

"Hell, yes, I've been drinking. I'm ready to party," he said loudly. "And you're not driving me anywhere. When Lane Turney takes a woman out, he does the driving . . . got that?" He staggered and stared, daring Lily to refuse.

She did.

"I'm not getting into the car with you in this condition," she said sharply, not caring who saw her predicament. "Please. You don't know what you're doing. Let me drive. I won't tell. I just can't ride with you like this."

The tremor in her voice was evident, but Lane couldn't have cared less about her fears or anyone else's safety, including his own.

"Fine," he said. "Then walk home. See if you can find someone else who'll look at that face long enough to give you a ride."

Lily turned her head away, refusing to give in to the pain of his words. They were nothing but the words of a drunk. They couldn't matter to her. Her life was what mattered.

"I'm sorry," Lily said to the bag boys who'd witnessed the entire episode. "Would you please push all this back inside out of the heat? I'll have to call the ranch for someone else to come."

They quickly pushed her purchases back inside with Lily close behind.

"Excuse me," a woman said, and put her hand on Lily's arm to get her attention.

Lily turned around to face one of the uniformed grocery checkers who'd been working on the aisle next to the one she'd used earlier.

"I couldn't help overhearing your troubles," the woman said. "My name is Debbie Randall. I know Case Longren and I know that he won't stand for this. I get off for lunch in ten minutes. If you don't mind waiting, I could run you home on my lunch hour."

Lily's eyes widened with surprise as the woman spoke, and then she sighed with relief as the answer to her predicament practically fell into her lap.

"That would be wonderful, Debbie," she said. She held out her hand. "My name is Lily. Lily Brownfield. I'm the new roundup cook at Longren Ranch."

The small, curvaceous woman gave Lily a quick but gentle once over, ignored the side of her face with studied aplomb, and then smiled. "I figured as much. Shoot. You'd be doing me a favor just to let me take you. That Case Longren is some hunk, hunh? I never pass up a chance to give him a hard time. Unfortunately, that's just about all he will let me hand out, if you know what I mean."

She laughed, deep and easy, and motioned for Lily to resume her seat on the stacked sacks of dog food.

Lily smiled back, watching with interest as the sexy little woman went back to finish her shift. She wondered as she watched her work if she and Case had ever dated, and then she wondered why she cared. It was none of her concern if Case Longren went to bed with every woman between here and the moon. She stifled the thought of Case . . . in bed . . . period. That man was too big and wild for her taste. That's what she kept telling herself all the way back to the Bar L.

THREE

Case came out the front door of his house, paused on the porch, and ran a hand through his thick, black hair. Frustration oozed. He kept trying to decipher the puzzle of why Lily left with someone other than Duff. But there were no answers shouting to be heard, only the bright, hot blue of a cloudless sky, a hummingbird darting in and out among the heavy, flowering morning glory vines on the trellis beside the porch, and the constant but distant lowing of cows searching for their newly weaned calves.

He sighed, jammed his hands deep into the front pockets of his Levi's, and kicked at a clod of dirt on the porch step with the toe of his boot. Dammit, he wished Lily would come down the driveway right now with that cool, touch-me-not expression and ease the worry in his belly. He looked long and hard toward the driveway and beyond, scanning the near-flat horizon. He saw nothing that would ease his mind.

The phone rang inside the house and Case spun around, letting the screen door bang sharply behind him as he hurried toward the den to answer it.

"Hello."

He yanked the receiver to his ear, hoping that the voice on the other end would be the same one who'd awakened him in the night two weeks earlier and turned his world upside down. But it wasn't Lily. And the caller did not have good news.

A station wagon belonging to the Longren Ranch had just been involved in a wreck on highway 183 north of Clinton. Case felt the bones in his legs turn to jelly as he sank backwards in his easy chair and closed his eyes. The deputy sheriff who was calling continued to relay his news.

"Is it bad?" Case whispered, and then cleared his throat, trying to swallow the panic that was setting in. "Were there any injuries?"

"Yes," the man began, "one. The ambulance is on the way to Clinton with the victim, but I don't know the extent of injuries."

Sweet Jesus, Case thought. He couldn't face the idea of Lily suffering anymore. She'd been through so much. And then it occurred to him . . .

"Is the injured person a man or a woman?" he asked sharply.

"Have no idea," came the reply. "I'll let you know more when I know more, Case."

"Yeah, right," Case answered. "And thanks a bunch for calling, buddy. You don't know how much this means to me."

Case hung up the phone. He was shaking and wanted to break something. He didn't know what to do first, head for town, or wait for the sheriff's call.

Lily!

Suddenly everything in his world just came into focus as he realized that she might no longer exist in it. The realization was not bearable. He hadn't known her much more than a week, but if he wasn't mistaken, he was falling in love with Lily Brownfield as surely as God made little green apples. If she was the one injured in the accident he might lose her before she ever knew she'd been found.

"Hey, Boss," Duff shouted through the screen door, unaware of the calamity that had just taken place. "Someone comin' down the driveway. Looks like that purty little grocery checker's car. What's her name . . . Debbie?"

Case staggered to his feet and wiped a shaky hand across his face. He didn't have time for visitors, especially persistent females no matter how pretty. He needed to get to the hospital now! He couldn't wait for the deputy's phone call. It might be too late.

"Oooh, goody," Debbie grinned. "The big man himself is waiting for us on the porch."

Lily's stomach gave a half-hitch and then settled back into position. Why did the sight of those broad shoulders, long legs and narrow hips give her such a jolt? She didn't even want to think about the expression on his face. It usually just made her nervous.

Case Longren always seemed to see right through her fake composure to the hurt and bitterness beneath. She didn't like that. It made her face what she'd become, and she didn't think she liked that either. Lily didn't used to feel sorry for herself. In fact she had frowned upon people who used their handicaps or personal tragedies to gain sympathy. Now she caught herself in the same frame of mind and knew she should be ashamed. She kept telling herself that there were many people who were much worse off than she. But every time she looked in a mirror that was hard to remember.

Debbie pulled to a stop right in front of the house and was out of the door, waving a cheery hello before Lily had time to comment.

"Hey, big man. You and Duff come give us a hand. I think Lily here just bought out the store."

Lily! Thank you, Lord! He didn't know why and he didn't know how, but he'd never been so relieved.

His legs worked all right. They carried him safely off the porch and all the way to the car toward Lily. But Debbie stepped in his path, forestalled his purpose, and promptly threw her arms around him, giving him a real, down-home hug.

"Hey, big man," she teased, "I haven't seen you at any of the local night spots in weeks. Have you taken a vow of celibacy I don't know about?"

Case turned at least three shades of red, and, still in Debbie's arms, he stared blindly over her head into the coldest green eyes he'd ever seen a woman wear.

"You're home," he managed to mumble at Lily.

"Obviously," Lily drawled, stared pointedly at Debbie's lush body plastered against him, and walked into the house with her arms full of sacks, leaving the others to follow suit.

"Don't be mad at her," Debbie teased. "She kinda got stuck between a rock and a hard place. I just offered her a bit of neighborly help. Didn't hurt that I'd get to see you, too."

Her words were brazen, but her heart was gold and Case knew it.

"I don't know why she's with you, but I'll owe you, Debbie Randall, for the rest of my life."

"Shoot," she grinned. "It's no big deal. Lily can tell you the whys and wherefores. I've got to head back, or I'll be late for work.

"Is that the last of the groceries?" Debbie asked, as Duff made his third trip to the car.

"Yep," he groaned, staggering from the weight and disappeared into the house.

"Then I'm off. Don't be a stranger, Case, honey," she called.

Case stood and watched Debbie disappear in a cloud of dust and then turned and walked toward the house.

"Debbie gone?" Duff asked, as he passed Case in the hallway.

"Yes," he answered. "And, Duff, I'll be out the rest of the day. See that everything runs smooth this afternoon. I have to run into Clinton. Probably won't be back until after dark."

"Gotcha," the tiny man waved, and stomped outside, his boots making a loud clump with each step he took.

Case walked into the kitchen, caught another cool look of disdain and wondered exactly what he'd done now to warrant all of this cold front. He was so glad to see her he didn't know where to start.

"I suppose you had your reasons," Lily began, "but next time I'd just as soon you sent someone else to take me shopping. Or better yet, let me go myself now that I know the way. I don't want to be within a county's distance of Lane Turney again. Do I make myself clear?''

Case's gut kicked. So it was Lane who'd wrecked and was on the way to the hospital. Somehow he should have known.

"I didn't send him," Case said quietly, frowning. No wonder she was angry with him. She thought he'd sent Lane to take her shopping, even after the way he behaved yesterday. *My God! Surely she knows me better than that?* The thought that she didn't trust him hurt all the way down.

"But he came," she argued. "He said you'd sent him to take me." And then her composure cracked and her bottom lip quivered as she stopped emptying grocery sacks and gripped the work island with shaky fingers. "And then he got drunk."

Case's loud expletive split the air, and Lily shuddered as she continued.

"Not at first. But afterward, when he came to the market to pick me up." Her words were stilted and coming faster and faster. Lily wrapped her arms around herself as if she were cold, and she began to pace between the counter and the cabinets. "I begged him to let me drive. He wouldn't."

"Honey," Case began. "It's all right. I know . . ."

"No," Lily interrupted. "You don't! I begged him. But he wouldn't let me drive . . . and I couldn't get in the car with him. He was drunk . . . and a drunk made me like this . . . and I . . ."

She was in his arms.

Case held her. She was shaking. Every breath she took was swallowed in a ragged gulp of fear.

"He had a wreck," Case said softly. "I thought you were with him. I've never been so afraid in my life, lady. All I could see was you, hurt . . . and it would have been my fault. I should have fired the son-of-a-bitch yesterday. If he hasn't killed himself, I still will.''

"Oh my God!" Lily moaned, and felt the ground tilting. Just the thought brought back every memory she had of the oncoming car that had swerved out of its own lane into hers and the ensuing pain and terror that had occurred. Somewhere daylight was disappearing beyond a wall of darkness and taking Lily with it. She went limp in Case's arms.

He felt her bones turning to jelly and knew he should have broken the news less suddenly, but it was too late now. He caught her before she hit the floor.

"Honey," he whispered against her ear. "I'm so sorry. Dear Lord, I'm sorry."

But Lily didn't hear him or see the look of love on his face as he carried her to her bed.

Case dashed into her bathroom and was back at her side, leaving little drips of water in his wake as he laid the cool, damp cloth across her forehead. His gaze feasted, knowing if she'd been awake, it would not have been allowed. He picked a long strand of hair from across her face, a gold thread from her crowning glory, and let it slide through his fingers before brushing it back into place. He smoothed the damp cloth down across her face, letting his finger run parallel to the scar that had sliced across her cheek and then leaned forward, kissing the corner of her mouth just below the end of the angry mark.

She moaned, and a sigh so soft it felt like the breath of an angel slid across his face. Case muttered softly and resisted the urge to lay himself down beside this woman and never let her go. He ran the cloth lightly down her neck, letting it rest for a moment against the rapid beat of her pulse that tap danced beneath his fingers and prayed that when she came to, she wouldn't blame him anymore than he blamed himself.

Her eyelids began to flutter, and Case leaned back, unwilling for her to know he'd been so close. It was a trespass she hadn't allowed, but it was one he wouldn't forget.

"Honey," Case said softly, "you're okay. You just fainted."

Lily opened her eyes, blinked several times in slow succession like a baby owl trying to focus, and when she did, she looked into the face of love. It was unmistakable, and it was on the wrong man. This wasn't Todd, and she wasn't back in L.A.

Suddenly the day's events came rushing back into her consciousness and she gasped, struggling to sit up and away from this big man who'd made her feel things she didn't want to remember existed. The expression she'd imagined disappeared as Case stood up and stepped back, allowing her the space she so obviously desired.

"I can't believe I did that," Lily said, as she smoothed at her hair with shaking fingers.

Her mouth trembled and her eyes watered, but she regained her composure in one fell swoop as she rolled away from him and off on the opposite side of the bed.

"Don't rush things," he said quietly, sadly watching the wall she was re-erecting between them. "You had a fright and, given your circumstances, a bad one. If you don't feel like it, you can skip the eve-

ning meal. We'll make do. The men have been o-
verfed since you came anyway.''

"Absolutely not," Lily said. "If you'll excuse
me, I'll just change out of my blouse and slacks into
my work clothes and get busy.'' She stood, giving
Case no choice.

He sighed, turned and fired the washcloth through
the bathroom door toward the sink. It slapped into
the basin with unerring aim, landing with a squishy
plop as he stomped out of the room without uttering
another word.

Lily blinked, puzzled by his near angry gesture
and wondered what was wrong with him. She was
the one who'd come close to being involved in another wreck. She closed the door behind him, shrug-
ging to herself about the mood swings of the big
cowboy. She slipped her blouse over her head and
stepped out of her slacks, then hung her clothing
back into the closet. She pulled a seersucker sundress
from a hanger and slipped it over her head. It was
older and would be cool to work in. She turned to
the mirror over her dresser, grabbed her hairbrush
and began pulling her long, silky hair into an orderly
twist that she pinned at the back of her neck. Then
she leaned forward, checking as she always did, to
see if the scar on the side of her face had disappeared
since she'd last looked. Lily frowned at the reflection. It was still there.

She started to turn away when the oddest thing
happened. Suddenly she no longer saw herself re-
flected in the mirror. She was looking at an instant
replay of Debbie Randall plastering herself into
Case's arms. She knew that she was finally allowing
herself to focus on something that had bothered . . .

no . . . shocked her, when she'd seen Case's arms wrap around another woman so easily. He'd held Lily the same way once, and she remembered liking it. She couldn't afford to become dependent on a man again. It hurt too much when it was over.

"What's wrong with you?" she snarled to herself in the mirror. "Wasn't one man's betrayal enough for you? What makes you think that another man would ever want to look at your face day in and day out for the rest of his life? Get a grip, Lily," she told herself, and slammed out of the room and into the kitchen as if the devil himself were at her heels.

Case was conspicuously absent at supper but Lily couldn't bring herself to ask his whereabouts. After the meal was over and the men had gone, she wandered throughout the downstairs portion of the house, trying to find something to do to occupy herself until she was exhausted and sleepy enough to go to bed.

She couldn't imagine why Case was absent. She supposed that she'd angered him with her rude, thankless behavior after he'd been so thoughtful and caring when she fainted. She refused to let herself remember the way he'd held her, whispering his thanksgiving that she hadn't been involved in the accident. She wouldn't remember the way it had felt to press against him, body to body, and mentally map every contour and plane of such a man as Case Longren. She wouldn't. She couldn't. It would hurt too much if she let herself care for anyone and then see that look of disgust she knew would appear when he looked at her face, knowing she'd never be pretty again.

Lily made a fist, slammed it against the side of her leg and mumbled to herself. This job was probably the worst idea she'd had in years, but she'd see it through. After all, she had nowhere else to go. She grabbed a couple of magazines from a table in the den and headed for her room.

Sometime later a knock on her bedroom door startled her and made her drop the magazine she'd been reading.

"Who is it?" she called, although she knew who was going to answer before the sound ever came. It was nearly ten o'clock and dark as pitch outside. None of the men would dare come in search of her at this time of night. It had to be Case.

It was.

"Me," he answered.

Lily opened the door and stared, trying not to give away the burst of pleasure she felt at just seeing him again.

"I thought you'd like to know that Lane is going to survive," he drawled. "At least he'll survive the accident. I can't vouch for what I'm going to do to him when he's dismissed from the hospital, and I can't say what the authorities are going to do to him for driving drunk, but I don't really give a damn. I just thought you might."

Pain opened and spread as Lily listened wordlessly to Case's almost angry recital.

"I'm glad he's okay," Lily answered. "And I thank you for thinking of me."

I always think of you, lady, Case thought.

"I'm sorry to be so much trouble," Lily mumbled, reading his behavior as angry and directed at her. "I suppose when you hired a long-distance cook, you never expected all this."

"I don't know what I expected," Case muttered. "But it wasn't you . . . and you're not trouble . . . and I'm thankful as hell that you're in my house, glaring at me, and building your walls to keep people out. For a short time today, I didn't think I'd ever get to say that, and I wasn't going to let another sun rise before I did. You can be mad. You can be offended. You can be any damned thing you please. And I don't care whether you like it or not, you're about to be kissed."

Lily was still trying to absorb what he'd just said when he hauled her into his arms and leaned toward her with intention in his eyes and love on his lips.

She knew just before their mouths merged that she'd been wondering what this would feel like ever since the first day she'd seen him dust-covered and weary, standing tall beneath the hot prairie sun.

The kiss.

At first it was tentative, a careful foray of nips and tastes that sent shivers spiking through the pit of Lily's stomach. Her hands knotted in the jacket he was wearing, and she inhaled as his mouth slid across her lips, seeking a firmer place to begin a more daring exploration. She drew his breath into her mouth and swallowed the groan that followed as Case slid his arms around her back and wrapped her so tightly against him she thought she'd just been melted and poured into his body.

"Oh God, lady," Case whispered, as he tore his mouth away from her open, inviting lips. "Make me stop before this goes any farther. You've got to because I don't think I've got enough guts to be a gentleman about this. I ache for more than you're ready to give."

Lily struggled with sanity, and slowly but surely pulled herself back together, withdrawing from Case's embrace with as much grace as she could muster.

"I don't think I'll ever be ready to give you what you want, Mr. Longren," she said coolly. "I don't hop in and out of men's beds."

Case was struggling with passion and fury as he grabbed Lily by the shoulders and shook her.

"I don't think I asked for anything casual, lady. In fact, I didn't ask for any damn thing at all except some sanity. You've taken away all of mine. I just thought you'd be willing to share some of your own. And don't think for a minute I'm going to forget that you kissed me back. You'd do well to remember it, too."

He turned and stalked away, disappearing into the shadowy darkness of the near-empty house with an ache in his heart and the pain that comes with unfulfilled passion.

Lily watched, dumbfounded by what had just transpired, and remembered, too late, that she was supposed to be the injured party here. She stepped back and slammed the door shut with a reverberating bang. But it was a bit too loud and a bit too late. Case had already torn a hole in the wall around her heart and left her empty and aching for more.

The next few days passed in a blur of revitalized activity. Another herd of cattle had been moved from their winter pasture back down to the ranch. The men were busy making steers out of the little bull calves, branding all the new livestock, and cursing the relentless sun and dust with every other breath. For spring, it was exceedingly hot.

Lily cooked, washed, cleaned, shopped and slept. Repeatedly. Her heart ached through the routine. Case hadn't done more than plaster her guilty conscience with several mind-boggling looks. They did nothing but remind her of how wonderful it had felt to be held in his arms. Then he would stomp outside with the rest of the men, keeping their contact to a minimum.

Nearly two hours had passed since supper was over and the last dish had been cleaned and put away. Lily was wandering through the house, searching for something to do. She didn't want to watch another television show. They were all reruns. She'd run out of anything new to read. And it was too early to go to bed. Besides, when she closed her eyes, all she could see was the look of pain on Case's face as he'd turned her loose and walked away. She couldn't let herself believe that she was anything more than a passing fancy . . . the only woman on the place syndrome. She'd convinced herself that no man would love her the way she was.

An owl hooted from a nearby tree, breaking the silence of oncoming nightfall, and Lily turned instinctively toward the door and the welcoming shadows of darkness. Night was comfortable to her. It was then that she looked the same as everyone else.

The air was a welcome twenty degrees cooler than it had been during the day. The nights were still quite cool and brisk, and a dew was falling. Lily could feel the air's dampness on her skin as she walked out onto the back porch and sat down in the porch swing.

It creaked, a gentle squeak every other push that reminded Lily she wasn't alone.

Case leaned against the fence outside the yard, secure that he was hidden in the darkness, and watched her swinging, leaning her head back and inhaling the scents and sounds of nightfall as readily as a woman born to the country.

She was a surprise, his L.A. woman. When she'd first arrived, he wouldn't have given a plug nickel for the bet that she'd last a week. But she'd fooled him. Hell, she'd fooled them all. Not only was she pretty, she was as capable as any hand Case had ever hired. And his arms ached to hold her as his body hardened with the need to make love to Lily all through the night.

Case swallowed a groan, pushed himself away from the fence and strode toward the porch, announcing his presence with firm steps.

Lily straightened immediately as she sensed someone coming up the path. She peered into the darkness and knew that the light from the kitchen behind her silhouetted her for anyone to see. A tiny sigh of relief escaped as she recognized the familiar shape of broad shoulders and long legs and that ever-present black Stetson crowning his head.

"Lily," he greeted, as he neared the porch.

"Case." She held her breath and waited.

He leaned on the porch rail and shoved his hat to the back of his head, waiting . . . hoping she'd say something more. She did not.

"I just thought you should know that I've decided to give the men a day off tomorrow."

"Why? Is something wrong? Are you already through with roundup?"

The panic in Lily's voice was evident, and it gave Case just the least bit of encouragement. She couldn't hate him all that much if she didn't want her job to come to an early end.

"No, honey," he said softly, ignoring her indrawn breath at the term of endearment. He didn't care. He was tired of letting her call *all* the shots. "One of the men got his foot stomped pretty good today. He'll be out for a bit, and several of the men are coming down with some kind of flu bug. I thought it'd be best if they all took a day's rest and let everything kind of get back to normal before we continued."

"Oh!" The relief in her voice spoke volumes.

"You can do whatever you want tomorrow. Sleep late, take one of the ranch vehicles and go to town and shop, whatever . . . I don't care. I only ask one thing of you. If you leave the ranch, let me know where you're going and an approximate time you'll be back. I at least want to know where to start looking if you don't show up on time."

"Yes, Father," Lily teased.

Case's heart jumped. She was smiling. He could see that much of her face in the shadows.

"I'm sorry," he grinned. "I didn't mean to come across so heavy-handed. It's just that you're fairly new to the area. I don't want you lost."

"Thank you," Lily said, in her most teasing ladylike manner. "It's nice to be wanted."

"Oh, you're wanted all right, Lily Brownfield. You have no idea how much."

Case walked past her and into the house, ignoring the look of consternation and then embarrassment that slid across Lily's face. Let her stew on that a while. He damned sure had.

* * *

Lily had gone nowhere. She'd opted for a lazy day in the sun and after sleeping to an unheard of nine o'clock in the morning, she'd skipped breakfast and gone outside with a glass of juice and a book she'd borrowed from Case's den. She stretched out on a chaise lounge in the sun.

Her long legs and arms were bare. The rest of her was indecently covered with a pink shorts and halter set, one that she'd have worn without a qualm back home on the beach. But here, she was a tiny bit nervous about someone seeing so much of her—especially since she was the only female within shouting distance among an unruly herd of men. She wasn't in fear for her life. Her heart was the only thing in danger. And Lily was slowly but surely admitting that to herself.

Case stood at the kitchen window and watched Lily reveling in her day in the sun. He supposed that she'd had many days like this back home in L.A. and wondered, not for the first time, if his dreams of keeping Lily Brownfield in Oklahoma were too farfetched.

She was not the usual country-girl type. She was city born, city bred, and educated to boot. He didn't know what made him so all-fired certain that she'd stay if he asked. He only knew that he wouldn't let her leave without giving it a try.

He heard the sounds of a vehicle coming down the long driveway and reluctantly turned away from the window overlooking the backyard. He went to the door and out onto the front porch, standing with one arm braced against the porch post as he watched a car full of men spill out of a dark sedan.

There was one older man, dark headed, two

younger men with matching hair and complexions, and two even younger men with hair as blond as Lily's. Something about the way they walked reminded him . . .

"Can I help you?" Case drawled, as they walked en masse toward him. He smiled to himself at the fancy he had of an imminent attack. They didn't look fearsome. In fact, they looked like they were in shock.

"Is this the Longren Ranch?" the older man asked.

"Yes," Case answered. "I'm Case Longren. What can I do for you?"

"We've come all the way from California to see Lily Brownfield. Is she here?" Morgan Brownfield asked, half expecting to hear him say no. He couldn't believe that his college-educated daughter was actually cooking for a roundup on an Oklahoma ranch. When he'd gotten her brief letter explaining what she'd planned to do, he'd been in shock. By the time the rest of his brood had been informed, they'd given Lily exactly three weeks to contact them. When she'd failed to do so, they'd come looking.

Case sucked in a breath. California! Please God, no!

"Yes, she's here," he answered. "But if one of you men is that sorry, fair-weather bastard of a fiancé, you can just take yourself all the way back to California and get off my property. Do I make myself clear?"

Cole Brownfield narrowed his dark eyes, grinning to himself as he watched his father's face. It looked like Lily had found one more man ready to fight for her honor. Somehow he wasn't surprised.

Morgan Brownfield couldn't think of what to say. With his abrupt, nearly rude dismissal of them, this man clearly had the same low opinion of Todd Collins that he had. It was such a surprise he was at a temporary loss for words. Finally he found his voice.

"Well, Mr. Longren. I don't know what else to say except that you're my kind of man. Hell no, I don't have that snake Collins with me. My name is Morgan Brownfield, and these are my sons, Cole, Buddy, and the twins, J.D. and Dusty. Lily is my daughter."

Case grinned wtih relief. He all but leaped off the porch with outstretched hand.

"Lily will be real glad to see you," he said. "And please, call me Case. Leave your things in the car, we'll get them later. Lily's out in the backyard. This is a slow day for the ranch, and I've given everyone the day off. You couldn't have come at a better time."

The last of Morgan's worries just flew off his shoulders. His first impression of this big, dark man was favorable, especially since he viewed Todd Collins with the same disdain. He wondered, for the first time, just how involved Lily might be with her boss, and looked at Case again, judging him anew.

"Our things are back in a motel in Clinton," Cole answered, as he stepped forward and shook hands. He sensed this man was going to make a difference in their lives.

"You can get them later," Case ordered shortly. "You're staying here. God knows there's plenty of room. It'll give you a better chance to visit with Lily."

The Brownfield crew wouldn't argue. They were

anxious to get a look at their beloved Lily. They rounded the house, following Case's lead. Cole was the first to spy his sister's familiar long legs stretched out on the lounger, soaking up sun.

"Lily Kate, you're the only person I know who'd leave California's sunny beaches and come to Oklahoma to get a tan."

That voice!

Lily flew from the lounge, dropped her book, and smiled.

The look on her face stopped Case's heart. My God, he'd give a year of his life if she'd look at him like that.

"Cole! Daddy!" her voice shook. "Oh my God! Buddy, J.D. and Dusty, too. You're here!"

She was engulfed.

FOUR

Morgan Brownfield watched Lily rearranging space for him and his sons in the eating area of the kitchen. She was moving chairs and brothers with expertise and abandon. If he couldn't still see the scar on her face, he'd swear that it was the same Lily he'd known and loved since the day she'd been born, not the withdrawn, silent woman she'd become after her accident and Todd Collins's betrayal.

He sighed quietly, relieved that Lily was healing in spirit as well as body. It was what he'd hoped and prayed for. And by the look on their host's face, it seemed as if he was partially responsible for Lily's sense of well-being. Case Longren never took his eyes off of her. In fact, he seemed to be mesmerized by Lily. Yet he stayed at a more than respectable distance away, obviously following boundaries that had been established long before the arrival of the Brownfield men.

Case watched every move Lily made, and missed

nothing of the amiable banter between her and her brothers, unaware that Morgan was watching him just as intently.

Lily was a completely different woman from the one who'd first arrived at the Bar L. She was tanned and smiling, and she no longer turned her face away at the slightest look. In fact, it seemed as if she'd almost forgotten the scar was there.

Case looked up, caught Lily's father staring at him, and hoped he didn't look as guilty as he felt. He also hoped that Morgan Brownfield couldn't see everything that was in his heart. It would be uncomfortable, to say the least, if Lily's father knew that he spent every waking moment wondering what it would be like to make love to his daughter.

"Lunch is ready," Lily called. "And just in time, here comes the crew."

Cole looked out the kitchen window and nearly forgot to breathe. Yesterday when they'd arrived, they'd had Lily all to themselves. But today it was business as usual, and he was dumbstruck by the rowdy crowd heading for the back door of the house.

"You mean you feed this many every day?"

"I feed them three times a day, goose," Lily teased. "It's no big deal. If you'd gotten up at a decent time this morning, you'd have met them then. It's just like feeding you guys only six times over. Sit down and mind your manners. I don't want the men to think I come from a family of heathens."

Case laughed. The look on her brothers' faces was priceless. They couldn't believe that Lily didn't think them perfect in every way. Their muttered complaints only heightened his laughter. He envied her the comfort of knowing that no matter what she said or did, she'd always have the love of her family.

Case was an only child, and his mother had left his father when Case was in college. It left him with nothing to come home to but a bitter, angry father who'd managed to maintain the ranch only long enough for Case to take over. After he had, Chock Longren had drunk himself into oblivion. As far as Case was concerned, his father had died years before his heart had actually stopped beating. He had no idea where his mother was and, quite frankly, had ceased to care. Lily was the first woman who'd mattered to him in a long, long while. Unfortunately, he had no idea how she felt about him. She alternated between being congenial but distant or ignoring him all together. He lay awake nights afraid that would never change.

Lily's family was greeted warmly by the outgoing bunch of cowboys and before long, they had talked her twin brothers, J.D. and Dusty, into trying their hand at helping brand and castrate the calves. The twins had decided that the experience would look great on their resumes.

Lily smiled. Knowing the twins, they'd succeed or die trying. They were the most competitive of her brothers, with each other, as well as everyone else they met. She pitied the poor calves until the Brownfields mastered the art of cowboying.

The meal was over. As usual, the men had eaten like a swarm of locusts. She was always amazed at the amount of food Case provided for them. He was a generous, as well as competent, boss.

She watched his interaction with her father and

brothers and knew that regardless of the geography that had separated their upbringings, they were remarkably alike: hardheaded but willing to listen, forceful and aggressive, yet compassionate. But the way Lily felt about Case was different from the way she felt about her family. She loved her father and brothers dearly, but the feelings she had when Case came close to her, the heat that splintered the ice in her heart when he turned his all-seeing, sky-blue gaze her way, had nothing to do with familial love. She didn't know whether it was a case of lust or the birth of something stronger, but Case Longren made her forget every ladylike manner she'd ever learned.

She closed her eyes and turned toward the mountain of dirty pots and pans, squelching the thoughts of Case right back where they belonged, in her twilight zone.

She waved a quick good-bye to the men as they stomped out the door and back to their jobs, taking her family with them. She didn't have time for frivolous thoughts. And she didn't intend to ever be put in a position for a man to hurt her again as Todd had done.

So it was shock that made her drop the pan full of soapy suds back into the sink, splashing water over the walls and down her front when a deep, husky voice drawled behind her.

"It's good to see you smile, Lily."

"For pete's sake, Case," Lily muttered, as she swiped uselessly at the soap and water dripping down from the cabinet onto the floor, "you startled me. I didn't know anyone was still here."

"Sorry," he said, but he lied.

He was not sorry he'd stayed behind, and he definitely wasn't sorry that the water that had soaked into the front of her blouse was making it almost translucent. He should have been. But he wasn't. Lily was so beautiful, and she curved in all the right places. He wanted to pull her into his arms and imprint himself into her body as persistently as the wet blouse that was sticking to her breasts.

"Just look what you've done," Lily accused, as she picked helplessly at the collar of her shirt.

"I'm looking," Case said, "but I'm not sure you'd be wanting me to if you could see what I see."

He struggled with the need to grin as Lily's face turned twelve shades of red and exploded into instant fury.

"If you were a gentleman, you wouldn't be looking," she blustered, and turned away in angry embarrassment.

"Oh no, Lily Catherine," Case said softly, "only a fool wouldn't look at a beautiful woman. Gentleman has nothing to do with it."

Lily forgot to breathe or argue with the fact that he'd taken to calling her by the name reserved for her family. Beautiful! Her hand shot toward her face in reflex to his words but it never reached the scar. Case caught it before it touched her cheek.

"I told you never to hide your face from me again, didn't I," Case said, as he threaded his fingers through her shaking hand and turned her in his arms to face him.

Lily nodded, although she refused to meet his gaze. She couldn't bear to see pity on his face.

But it wasn't pity that Case wore, and Lily should have looked.

"I almost forgot why I came back," Case said softly, tilting her head up to meet his look. "Don't cook tonight. Set out some sandwich fixings. The men can fend for themselves. I'm taking you and your family out to eat."

The pleasure that shot through her died almost as quickly as it was born. She hadn't been out socially in public since her accident and the panic that followed the pleasure made her stiffen in Case's arms.

"I don't think that's such a . . ."

"I didn't ask you what you thought, Lily. I don't even want to hear it. I'm not asking anything of you that you're not ready to face. It's not like I asked anything so difficult of you. I could have asked you to my bed, Lily. But I didn't. I only asked you to dinner. Please . . ."

If he just hadn't mentioned his bed she wouldn't have forgotten to be angry. It was the image his words painted that made her forget what she'd been about to say. But he had, and she folded in his arms like an umbrella in a windstorm. She shrugged.

"You could ask, Case Longren, until your tongue fell out, but bed is the last place I'd go with you." The expression of cool disdain she was trying to effect was failing miserably. "However, since you said please, I suppose dinner isn't out of the question . . . as long as my father and brothers are along."

Case grinned. When he left, she was going to be furious with him as well as herself, but he'd take what he could get and for now, dinner was it.

''That's the most ladylike insult I've ever received, Lily love.''

He leaned forward, his mouth opening, opening, and then Lily watched in shocked fascination as it pursed. Case took a deep breath and blew long and slow at the soap bubble hanging suspended on the side of her face. It lifted off her cheek and floated into the air at eye level where Lily saw Case stick out a finger and burst its errant flight. The tiny pop it made was almost nonexistent, but Lily heard it just the same. At least she thought it was the bubble, but it might have been one of the icicles breaking away from her heart. She wasn't sure, and she didn't want to find out.

''So you're having a barbecue Saturday night?'' Lily's brother Buddy asked between mouthfuls of salad he was shoveling into his mouth with less than precision.

It was the first Lily had heard of any barbecue and she alternated between panic at the amount of food she would have to prepare and the fact that Buddy needed his manners cleaned up. She'd been away from home too long.

''Buddy, you still haven't lost it, have you?'' Lily asked sharply.

Her brother looked up, the question hanging from his eyes as accurately as the string of lettuce hanging from his mouth.

''Lost what?'' he mumbled.

''The ability to talk and chew at the same time,'' Lily drawled.

Buddy blushed and shoveled the bit of lettuce inside with the rest as he grinned at the good-natured banter he was receiving.

"Sorry, sis," he said. "I guess you need to come back home more often and give us a refresher course on manners. There's too many men living in that big old house alone."

"That's not my fault, brother dear," Lily teased. "I still can't fathom why four perfectly healthy men haven't been able to find just one woman between you. You're either all awfully selfish and set in your ways, or there's something you guys haven't told me about your choice of life-styles."

Case burst out laughing at the look of indignant shock that flew around the table. Lord, it must be nice to have such a family! And he wished with all his heart that he was a part of it.

"I don't think any of us have anything to apologize for," Cole muttered. "We just haven't found the right woman yet, just like you hadn't found the right man, Lily Kate. You know we all hated Todd 'The Bod' from day one. We weren't far off the mark on him, so there's still hope for us . . . and for you, too." Then he grinned and looked pointedly at the big man sitting to her left.

Lily flushed and looked down at her plate. She knew they were right. She'd never guessed so wrong about a man in her life. And that was one reason she didn't trust her budding emotions about her boss, either.

She glanced nervously around the crowded restaurant, smoothed at the bodice of the pink silk sheath she was wearing, and imagined that everyone was staring at her disfigured face. She breathed a tiny sigh of relief when she could see no one looking in their direction. She started to slide her hand up to her cheek when she remembered Case's warning and turned wide, green, shell-shocked eyes toward him instead.

Sure enough, hot blue was watching her every movement as intently as a spider watches a daredevil fly. Glaring at his temerity, she tilted her head back in defiance, unaware of the seductiveness of the movement as the curls clouding around her neck fell down her back and over the top of the chair in which she was sitting.

Case caught his breath as he watched her hair slide like hot honey over and down the furniture and wished they were somewhere alone. He'd take off every stitch of clothing she was wearing and clothe her in nothing but that abundant, glorious gold.

Lost in thought, he almost missed it as Lily's father chided Cole for mentioning Todd Collins at all.

"You didn't have to bring that up," Morgan said angrily.

"No, Dad," Lily said. "It's all right. And he's right. What can I say? As J.D. always says, I was suckered."

Case watched the hurt come and go in her eyes and wished he had the right to take her in his arms and heal the pain. But he didn't and had to satisfy himself with less.

Lily caught her breath and let her mouth fall open in slight surprise as Case slipped his hand beneath the tablecloth, pulled the napkin from her hand, and threaded his fingers through hers.

He'd known, even with all her laughter and teasing, that she was still hurting. He'd heard the bitterness in her words just as he now felt the anger.

Lily looked up and saw the expressions on his face flash and flare as his work-roughened palm slid across her smaller, softer one, engulfing it in a strong, sensuous stroke of comfort.

Morgan caught the look that passed between them and wondered if Lily was just getting out of one problem and into another. They knew little about Case Longren other than the fact that he was successful and hard-working and seemed to worship the ground Lily walked on. But Todd Collins had those traits and look what he'd done! However, there was one thing in Case's favor. He didn't seem to be aware of the long red scar down Lily's face. In fact, he didn't act like he even knew it was there.

Morgan sighed. He knew that it did no good to worry. His daughter was grown and could and would make her own decisions. He just prayed that it wouldn't get her hurt again.

"So," Buddy continued as if nothing else had ever been said, "what's with the barbecue?"

Case grinned as he answered.

"It's kind of an annual tradition. Neighbors come bringing everything good to eat and I furnish the meat. Duff, my foreman, is an expert when it comes to outdoor cooking. Usually we help him with the calf fries, but the side of beef is his priority."

"Calf fries?" Lily hadn't heard the term before but the answer she received did nothing to assure her that she was ever going to let a morsel of it pass her lips.

"You mean you eat . . . you cook what was . . . people actually want to eat what was once . . ." laughter was rising around the table as she continued in shocked horror, ". . . the reproductive organs of poor unfortunate animals?'' Lily gasped and pressed her fingers to her lips.

"Oh God! Lily, you're priceless.'' Case couldn't contain his mirth. ''That's the most ladylike description I ever heard put to . . .''

Lily interrupted him before he could finish.

"I don't eat such things, and I can't imagine anyone else doing so either.'' Her indignation was rising.

Case leaned back in his chair in full view of everyone in the restaurant and let a full belly laugh flow forth. He couldn't help it. His L.A. woman was suddenly out of her depth in more ways than one.

"Remember when I was afraid you'd feed my men sunflower seeds?'' Case said, trying to pull himself together. ''Well, why don't you just look at calf fries as . . . hamburger seeds? After all, if they'd stayed where nature intended, somewhere down the road they'd have been responsible for hamburger. What do you think?''

"I think you're all full of bull,'' Lily said distinctly, as she rose and excused herself from the table. ''And I think I should go powder something . . . or,'' she mumbled as she walked away from the table, ''take a powder. It might be safer. I'm definitely outnumbered tonight.''

The next few days saw increased activity as the roundup got back in full swing and preparations for the barbecue began. Lily was relieved that the night would amount to an evening off for her. She didn't have the usual mountain of food to prepare, only some fruit pies as her contribution to the buffet.

She'd refused point blank to have anything to do with cooking the small, oval, milky-white slices that would ultimately result in the famous calf fries.

Just remembering their origin made her wince. Poor animals! It did no good to listen to Case's patient explanations about the futility of having too many bulls on the same ranch and the dangers of inbreeding that could result. It just wasn't something she was comfortable discussing. Now if they'd wanted to discuss the stock market instead of the beef market, she'd have been more confident. But she was in the wrong place and the wrong state for such matters. Oklahoma was definitely more than a state of the union, it was a state of mind.

"Lilleee!" Buddy's bawl echoed down the long staircase and throughout the downstairs area with persistent pathos.

She rolled her eyes, dusted the flour from her hands, and eyed the fruit pies. They were at a safe stage to leave for a few minutes. From the sound of her brother's call, he was in some sort of difficulty. However, with Buddy, it wasn't always easy to tell.

She started throught the wide, spacious downstairs, letting her eyes feast on the old-fashioned, almost Victorian look the house wore and knew that nothing had been changed or redecorated since Case was a child. But she liked it. It was always clean, open and inviting, and she wished she had an excuse to venture through it more often. Case had a professional cleaning crew who came weekly. They did their job, stayed out of Lily's way when she was busy, and disappeared as quietly as they appeared.

At first the presence of two men and one woman who moved throughout the house in their crisp green coveralls like garden shadows was disconcerting. But now she took them as a matter of course and was grateful for the fact that all she had to do was cook. The house was enormous and almost more than one person could have managed. It was a shame that Case lived in it alone.

"Lilleee!" Buddy repeated, only louder and longer.

She took the stairs in double-time.

"Coming," she called, and met him ambling out of his room with a shirt in one hand and a string tie in the other.

"What's wrong now?" she asked with a grin, as her beloved Buddy shoved both objects toward her with a panicked look on his face.

"The top button is off, and I don't know how to tie this tie."

"Lord love a duck, Buddy. I thought you were being killed or something."

Buddy grinned helplessly and shrugged.

Lily's sigh was one of loving disgust.

Buddy was the second oldest, but the least able to cope with problems. He lived in a world of computers and machines that didn't allow the human connection. He was a computer programmer and just shy of brilliant. But he was the least likely to ever marry. He evaded personal relationships like the plague and the only female allowed in his world was his baby sister, Lily.

"Something wrong?" Case asked, as he burst through the bathroom door with nothing on save an oversized bathtowel.

Oh God! I didn't need to see this. I know I won-

dered if he was brown all over, but I really didn't want to know. Now how am I going to forget?

"Ooops," Case grinned, and grabbed at the twist of towel at his waist, just to make sure that it was still secure. "I didn't know you were up here, Lily. I was in the shower and heard someone yelling over the racket the water was making. Thought someone was in trouble."

Yes, someone is in trouble now, if they weren't before, and the someone is me, Lily thought.

"Sorry," Buddy said. "Button off, can't tie my tie."

Case grinned at the look of shock Lily was wearing and then swallowed the seed of hope that burst forth as he saw something more spreading across her face. If he wasn't dreaming, it looked a bit like interest. In fact, it might even be described as . . . intrigue.

"There's needle and thread on the top of my dresser," Case said, as he started back into the bathroom. "And a button box beside it. Help yourself, Lily. As for his tie, when he's ready to put it on, I'll help him. Can't have this L.A. man out of step tonight. Too many pretty ladies coming."

Buddy looked like he'd swallowed a worm. Women?

"Give me the darn shirt," Lily grumbled, and yanked it out of his hand before he could think of an argument for not attending the barbecue.

Buddy ducked back into his room.

Lily let him go, but she knew it would take more than food to get him back out again. Case shouldn't have mentioned the women. Lily knew all about Buddy's nervousness because she felt it herself. She needed to get away from the sight of Case . . . and all that tan skin . . . those long muscular legs and arms . . . that damn towel . . . and what she couldn't see.

She flew into his room and then stopped in mid-step. She'd never been past the door, and the shock of his bed was more than she'd been prepared for. It was the biggest, tallest four-poster she'd ever seen. And the bedspread! It was black satin, and Lily had never been so entranced in her life. This dirt and no-nonsense cowboy slept beneath black satin?

Her hands were shaking as she grabbed the thread from the dresser and unwound a length from the spool before biting it from the bolt. The images that kept springing to mind did nothing to help her thread the needle she'd confiscated from the pincushion. She slipped the end of the thread into her mouth and then pulled slowly, carefully wetting the end of the fiber before trying to slide it into the tiny eye of the needle.

Case watched her look of intense concentration and growing frustration as she kept missing the eye. He couldn't take his sight from the way she kept snaking her tongue out to catch the end of the errant thread and redampening it before trying to slide it back through the needle. My God the thoughts that tongue evoked!

"Need any help?" he asked quietly.

Lily jumped. The needle fell to the floor and the button she was holding rolled under the dresser.

"Dammit," she muttered in unladylike fashion, as she dropped to the floor on her hands and knees, retrieved the needle, and began feeling around for the button. "I wish you'd quit sneaking up on me."

Lily felt the button about the same time she saw

his bare feet and jean clad legs step up beside her. She grabbed it between her fingers, turned around and took the hand he offered as she pulled herself up. The problem she now faced was the fact that jeans were all he was wearing.

Lily was staring point-blank at the broadest, brownest, chest she'd ever seen in her life. Her eyes kept trying to look upwards to Case's face, but she couldn't seem to get past all that bare skin.

"Find it?" he asked with a grin, knowing full well how much his presence was addling her.

"It?" Lily asked inanely.

"The button . . . or whatever it was you dropped," he asked.

"Oh . . . button . . . here."

She held it up for proof and then felt like crawling under that black-satin covered bed and never coming out again. He was laughing at her. Her hand went automatically toward her face, but the look that came in Case's eyes warned her she should have thought before she touched.

"I told you never to hide your face from me again, didn't I, Lily?"

She started to argue. She may as well have decided to run for president. Both were futile.

Case took the needle from one hand, the button from the other and replaced them on his dresser with overdone caution.

"No weapons," he muttered, just before he swooped.

Lily was engulfed in warm skin, strength, and the sound of the wildest beating heart she'd ever felt against her cheek.

"What do you think you're doing?" she managed to whisper.

"No talking," he muttered again.

"Case?"

It was the last word Lily uttered.

He captured her hands and pulled them around behind him, coaxing her to hold on. She did, for dear life. His mouth marauded across her face until it came to her lips and fixed with precision across their softness like a drowning man searching for a pocket of air.

His body tensed, waiting for the explosion that never came. When he felt her arms wrapping around his waist, as she actually pulled herself closer against him, a low, agonized groan was all he could manage. She was kissing him back! He'd never wanted anything so much, or been so sorry he'd started something he couldn't finish in his life. In less than an hour, people would start arriving for the barbecue, never mind the fact that Lily's father and four brothers were just beyond his door. God in Heaven, this was going to kill him!

Case ran his hands lightly down her shoulders, letting them brush suggestively against the sides of the breasts that strained against his chest, and then he cupped the span of her waist before pulling them apart.

"You're the first thing on my mind every morning, and the last thing every night, Lily, love. But as God is my witness, I can't let this go any farther or your family will hang me like a dog in front of all the company that's coming."

Lily shuddered at the ache she felt when Case released her, and ducked her head, suddenly ashamed that she'd welcomed him so openly without the slightest argument. He must think she was desperate.

"I'm sorry," she mumbled.

"Don't you be sorry," Case growled, and grabbed her hand before sliding it slowly down his belly toward the aching bulge behind his zipper. "As you can tell, I'm the one who's sorry. But it won't always be like this between us, Lily. Not if you'll let me show you that some men can be trusted."

Lily blushed, and started to snatch her hand away, when something made her hesitate. Instead she slid it back up the front of his belly to rest on the wild heart beating beneath her palm.

"Trust is not what this is about," she said quietly. "It's about what I see every time I look in a mirror and about the first thing you would see when you woke up with me beside you. That's what this is about, Case."

She turned away, carefully retrieved her needle, thread and button and her brother's shirt, and walked out of the room without another word.

"If I ever get the chance," Case muttered to himself as he stared at the closing door, "I think I just may have to break Todd Collins's damn neck."

Lily's apprehension disappeared beneath the laughter and dust of the constant stream of people arriving and food being distributed to the various tables set up beneath the shade trees in the front yard. A hint of the cooking beef and the smoke of the hickory fire beneath it drifted through the waning heat of the day. Before long sunset would arrive and with it the welcome shadows of night that would give her some measure of security.

She and her family were introduced constantly to the people who kept coming in droves until finally

Case left them to make their own introductions to the few stragglers who came late.

Lily saw several double takes toward her face, but not one snicker or unkind word drifted to her ears. It wasn't horror, or shock, but merely a kind curiosity for the obvious tragedy she'd suffered. No one asked, and Lily didn't offer an excuse and finally it was almost forgotten. Only now and then did Lily remember that she was branded just like those newly weaned calves still bawling in the corrals beyond the main house.

"Come and get it," Duff bellowed, and his tiny stature disappeared in the melee that ensued.

The Brownfields were impressed by the open, friendly manner with which they were received and knew that no matter what else, Lily was definitely in the right place for her spirit to heal. They'd never met so many people who accepted them on face value.

Cole Brownfield watched with interest as even his reticent brother, Buddy, became engrossed in a conversation with a serious young woman who'd plopped down beside him to eat her meal. He was amazed. The woman must be something. Buddy wasn't wearing his usual panicked look. If this had been a party back in L.A., Cole knew he would have already had to admit to being a police officer, watched the look of judgment come and go that always followed, and either been propositioned or ignored. Here nobody cared or judged. He was just accepted as Lily's older brother. Or so he'd imagined until he was introduced to a little bitty piece of womanhood named Debbie Randall. With her, he'd been appraised and found wanting.

She'd enchanted Morgan, set Buddy at ease, and all but squealed with delight when she'd discovered that J.D. and Dusty were into acting. Women! It figured! She'd barely acknowledged his presence after that. And it was just fine with him. He didn't need small, Oklahoma twister-type ladies on his heels. He had enough to deal with just worrying about his sister.

He kept one eye on the festivities, enjoying himself with the friendly banter, and the other eye on Lily who tried with little success to withdraw into shadows. Case Longren wouldn't let her and for that, Cole was glad. He liked the big cowboy, and knew that if Lily would let it, a serious relationship could develop quite easily.

"What do you think, Dad?" Cole asked his father as Morgan wandered by in search of a refill for his quart-sized tea glass.

"I think I'll be hunting antacid tablets about midnight, but I've never tasted so much good food in one place." He grinned and patted his stomach.

"I mean about Lily," Cole said.

Morgan turned and stared at his daughter. She was almost leaning against Case's chest as she laughed at something Duff said, and then her laugh was stifled as one of the twins walked by and shoved a huge bite of barbecue in her mouth. The ruckus that ensued was a welcome sight. When Lily left California, she not only wouldn't have been laughing in such a crowd, she would not have retaliated toward her brother as she had.

"I think she's just about healed inside," Morgan said quietly. "But I don't know if she's going to be able to live with the way she's healed outside."

"I think the man standing behind her can do it for her, Dad. When we leave, don't give her any unnecessary words of advice this time. Let Lily make her own decisions without giving her any outs as to coming back and staying with us."

Morgan turned and looked at his eldest son with a look of shock.

"Do you know what you're saying?" he asked sharply.

"I not only know, I'm bucking for the guy," Cole answered. "Just look at the way he watches her, Dad. If he doesn't already love her, he's so damn close it makes no difference."

Morgan nodded and stared, yet he could not stop the little twinge of worry that crept into his chest. Lily had suffered so much. He couldn't bear it if there was more to follow.

"I hear you, Cole. And I'll follow your lead . . . this time. But God help the man who ever hurts Lily again."

"You don't have to tell me, Dad," Cole said quietly. "I'm the one you had to stop from going to L.A. and rearranging Todd Collins's face, remember. I don't care how old she is, she's still *my* baby sister."

Case watched Lily slip away from the festivities and head toward the house. She hurried up the porch steps and entered the back door without looking back. He tossed his near empty plate in a trash barrel and followed just as the first strains of "Shenandoah" drifted through the air. Pete was playing his fiddle.

"Lily!" he called aloud, as he entered the kitchen.

Her quick reappearance surprised him. "What do you need?" she asked, as she entered the room carrying a lightweight jacket. "Are we out of ice? Should I make some more lemonade?"

Case stopped. "Where did you go?" he asked.

"I was getting chilly. I went to get a jacket."

"Oh! I thought . . . never mind what I thought," Case muttered. He didn't want her to think he'd expected her to hide from all the strangers.

"What are we running out of?" Lily asked, and started toward the door.

"Patience," came the quiet answer.

Lily blushed.

Case could see the flush spreading across her face and knew that he should resist. It was no use.

"Come here," he urged, and wrapped Lily in his arms.

"Case," she muttered, "someone will see."

"See what?" he growled. "All they'll see is you and me . . . dancing. What's so wrong with that?"

"Dancing?" And then Lily heard Pete's fiddle and the poignant melody drifting into the open doorway. "Oh! Dancing."

"May I?" Case asked softly as he released her and took a step back, offering his hand as he awaited her decision.

Lily took a deep breath, knew that she might regret this later, but could no more refuse him than stop the wind from blowing. "I'd be honored," she whispered.

She stepped into his arms, laid her cheek against his chest, and waited. He swung her into a waltz, their feet moving in perfect unison as he led, and

Lily followed. Right then Lily would have followed him to hell and back if that's where he'd been going.

The music was old, the melody sweet, and Lily's breath caught in her throat as Case turned and dipped, swirling them through the kitchen and out onto the back porch where the music was blended with song as one of the men softly sang the accompanying words to Pete's concerto. Back and forth, up and down, they dipped and swayed across the porch, lost in the shadows and the mood of the night.

His breath brushed against her ear and Lily bit her lower lip to keep from turning toward his mouth in desperation. She didn't want to be attracted. She didn't want to hurt again. She didn't want to need to lie down beneath this man . . . but she did. *Can he feel my heart race?*

Does she know how much I want her? Can't she tell how bad I ache?

Lily sighed, and stepped closer. Case held his breath and pulled her into his arms. The music still played, but their feet had long since ceased movement. Lily looked up into blue so pure it took her breath away. She started to speak, but the words never came. They were lost in the groan that followed Case's lips as he swept across her mouth in total abandon.

Suddenly there was nothing but Case's hands on her body, his mouth on her lips, and her feet off the ground. Case swung her up and turned until she was pressed against the wall of the house as he buried himself in the softness of Lily.

He shook. She was soft, and warm, and she'd allowed him more than he would ever have dreamed. And it was not enough.

"Lily . . ." he groaned quietly.

"No," she answered, before he could ask.

He sighed. He slid her down against him until her feet touched the porch, brushed the tangle he'd made of her hair away from her face, and leaned his chin against the top of her head.

"Someday you won't tell me no, Lily Catherine."

Her heart twisted from the pain in his voice, but the conviction with which he spoke gave her hope. If she could only believe him. If she could only believe in herself.

FIVE

Lily brushed a light swath of blush across each cheek and tried not to frown at the slash beneath. It was Sunday. Her father and brothers were still here. Their presence had given her the courage to do something she'd been wanting to do ever since her arrival. She was going to church. But she wasn't going alone.

She smiled, remembering the look of shock on Case's face last night when she'd announced her intentions.

"Church? Me?"

Lily stared, calmly waiting for the shock to lessen. When she thought he was ready, she continued.

"Yes, you . . . and me . . . and my family. Back home I never missed." She fixed him with a look that made him fidget as she pressed the issue. "Don't you attend?"

"I used to," he said shortly. "But that was years

ago . . . when my parents were still together. I haven't been in a long . . ."

Lily nodded. "I suspected as much. It's high time you did." And then she softened her remark with an innocent question. "Don't you think so?"

Case stuffed his hands in his pockets. Her Madonna-like expression wasn't fooling him. She *was* quiet. He'd give her that. And she was *always* a lady. That was obvious. But he suspected where will was concerned, hers was forged of iron. It was just the covering that was deceptive.

"I think you're right, Lily," he said quietly. "It's high time a lot of things happened around here. I'll be ready when you are."

Lily knew that her announcement had just taken second place to what he'd implied. The *things* that Case Longren wanted to happen involved her and she knew it. The problem was, she wasn't ready to deal with problems, of any kind.

"It's getting late," Lily called, standing at the foot of the stairs as she watched the first of the Brownfield men ambling down.

Her father was at the head of the line. He, too, was in the habit of attending church back home in Laguna Beach. He welcomed the chance to sample religion, country-style.

The twins came next, blond, California-tan, and flashing green eyes. As always, dressed alike in co-ordinating colors, their shirts and slacks would probably cause a stir in the congregation, especially if there were any unattached females around.

Cole sauntered down behind them, one hand on the bannister, the other coaxing their brother, Buddy, to pay attention to where he was walking and put away the hand-held computer game with which he was fiddling.

"Give it to me," Lily said quietly, as Buddy's foot hit the bottom step.

He looked up, surprised to see where he was and started to argue. He never went anywhere without one of his computers. But the look in her eyes was not to be denied. He sighed and handed it over.

Case watched from the top of the landing, smiling softly at the competent but loving manner with which Lily treated her family. They all looked to her for assurance and confirmation that they were presentable. He suspected that her mother's death years ago had thrust her into a very responsible position at an early age.

Lily counted heads. There was one missing. She turned back to the stairs and started to shout when she saw him standing above her, staring down.

Her pupils dilated. Whatever she'd been about to say was wiped from her mind by those clear blue eyes. Her fingers tensed and then clenched into fists as she watched him begin to descend the stairs. Every step he took pulled the soft brown fabric of his dress slacks against hard, muscled thighs. The scent of shoe polish came down with him and Lily knew that his boots had suffered a much-needed cleaning in her honor. The muscles in his arms corded as he reached behind his neck and adjusted the collar of his shirt. He took the rest of the stairs two at a time.

Lily tried to remind herself that it was Sunday. She was supposed to be in a godly frame of mind. To contemplate the week's past transgressions and hope for a better future. But the sight of that man and those all-seeing eyes gave her thoughts that didn't belong in church. She spun around, leaving him to descend the last few steps unobserved.

Case saw the flags of color sweeping across her cheeks and knew it was more than the makeup she was wearing. It did his heart good to realize that even in some small way he was getting to her. It was only fair. She'd been getting to him ever since the day she'd arrived.

"Who's riding with whom?" Cole asked with interest, missing nothing of the looks his sister and her boss had exchanged.

Before Lily could argue, Case took the matter out of her hands.

"Lily can ride with me. The rest of you follow along behind. That way no one will be crowded and we'll arrive in passable condition. How does that sound?"

"Sounds good to me," Morgan said, and headed out the front door with his sons following along behind like a covey of quail.

"You did that on purpose," Lily accused.

"I know it," Case said.

It took the air out of her complaint. She hadn't expected him to own up to it. "Well then," she huffed. "We'd better hurry or we'll be late."

"Yes, ma'am," he said quietly.

They made a dusty convoy as they turned left at the crossroads outside of Clinton.

"Where are we going?" Lily asked. She'd expected the services to be held in the town proper.

But it was obvious that Case was turning in another direction.

"To church," he answered. "It's the one where I was baptized. I suppose that's where you wanted to . . ."

"It's fine," she said softly, trying not to think about Case and babies within the same heartbeat.

And then the small country church came into view, nestled beneath the only stand of trees for miles. The closer they came, the quieter Case got. Lily almost wished she hadn't pressed this. She could tell that this was difficult for him. *From the look on his face, it should have happened years ago.*

Case searched the dusty, white exterior. Nothing had changed. The hand-painted sign at the foot of the steps swung on rusty chain links from an equally rusty iron post. The crepe myrtle bushes beneath the windows were still scraggly and trying to bloom, just as they had every summer since he could remember. Western Oklahoma was too dry for most shrubs to thrive. But the people thrived just as they had since statehood. On hard work and determination not to let the flat, often too-dry land get the best of them.

"We're here," Case announced unnecessarily.

"You're a Methodist." The statement was said with some surprise, but with a sense of satisfaction. "So am I."

"Something in common," Case said quietly, letting himself absorb her beauty and tranquility. And then he watched her hand slip up the side of her face and knew that she was nervous about meeting strangers.

He threaded his fingers through her hand and

coaxed. "Come on, Lily. This is going to be good for both of us."

That the congregation stared was putting it mildly. That they quickly regained their sense of balance and calmly scooted closer in the pews to make room, said something for their down-home, matter-of-fact lifestyle.

Lily imagined that everyone was looking at her. But the longer she sat, the more apparent it became that her brothers were the center of attention. She'd been right in assuming they'd be a hit with the unattached females in the area. It was something when one single man hit town running. When four came in one fell swoop, it was not to be ignored. And the Brownfield men were definitely not being ignored.

J.D. and Dusty were comfortable with being stared at. Because they were twins, it had always been part of their life. Buddy had panicked. But it was to be expected. Women always made him nervous. He'd quickly taken a seat between Lily and his father. Cole was the one who was trying to maintain his composure. But the impish face of Lily's friend, Debbie Randall, looking at him from the pew across the aisle, had given him second thoughts about bolting for cover as any smart cop would do.

"And the Lord said . . . 'Thou shalt not commit adultery' . . ."

The minister's voice rose with vehemence. He nearly shouted the commandment to the congregation.

Cole jumped and then tried to cover his movement by straightening his slacks. *Guilty conscience*, he thought with a wry smile, and forced all thoughts of Debbie Randall's dark brown eyes out of his mind.

Case let his arm slide along the back of the pew and resisted the urge to cup Lily's shoulder and scoot her closer against him. Adultery and Lily Brownfield didn't even belong in the same sentence. His thoughts of his cook had nothing to do with lust . . . and everything to do with love.

He'd sat on the scarred side of her, subconsciously putting himself between Lily and the congregation. He felt her tension. But the longer they sat, the more she relaxed. And then finally, he could tell when she forgot about everything except the message the minister was delivering.

A shaft of sunlight pierced the small, stained glass window behind the pulpit and beamed toward him as if on a heavenly mission. He tried not to fidget, but he was curious as to where the light had stopped. Finally, he allowed himself a quick glance. He didn't have far to look.

In her hair, in the crown of gold braid fastened high on her head, was a rainbow of color from the window's patchwork of lead and colored glass. Blue as clear as the sky outside, gold that blended into the luster of her own hair, red as dark as the blood on the cross, and green as true as Lily's eyes.

Case forgot to breathe. Tears quickened and he quickly blinked them away. It hadn't taken long that morning to fall in love. Now all he had to do was convince Lily to follow suit.

"Let us pray," the minister said solemnly.

Case was the first to obey. He had plenty to pray about.

* * *

The congregation was filing out the door, quietly visiting with each other and catching up on the week's events as they waited their turns to shake hands with the preacher.

Debbie stepped up behind Cole Brownfield and knew that, for the moment, he was unaware of her presence. It gave her a little time to appreciate the broad sweep of shoulders beneath his pale green shirt and admire the long legs filling out his navy blue slacks.

"Hi," she finally whispered, and smiled with hidden relish as he visibly jerked.

"Oh!" Cole muttered, swiveling quickly to see who was talking. "It's you."

"Nice service, wasn't it?" she asked, and let herself be joggled against his backside by the people crowding behind her, anxious to get outside and home to their waiting dinner.

Cole bit his lip to keep from swearing as he felt her breasts push against his backbone. *Damn woman. She'd try the patience of a saint.* And then he acknowledged with a weak sigh, *And I'm no saint.*

"It was fine," Cole said shortly and prayed that that was daylight up ahead he saw.

Debbie smiled again. This was the best sermon she'd ever heard. She was heartily glad she'd come to church this morning. *To think, I almost didn't come,* she thought. And then she wondered, as the minister came into view, *What in the world did he preach about today?* All she could remember was something about one of the commandments. She'd been lost after she'd seen the visitors entering the sanctuary. *Oh well, it'll be enough to remark upon.*

"Great sermon, Brother Donald," Debbie said, as

she clasped the preacher's hand and pumped it heartily.

At least one of the congregation was listening this morning. After the new arrivals had taken their seats, he'd felt himself losing their attention. Brother Donald beamed.

"Case, it's sure good to see you here this morning."

Lily recognized a neighbor from a nearby farm who'd been at the barbecue the other night. She smiled self-consciously and started to turn her head to the side when Case grabbed her gently by the elbow as he included her in the welcome.

"It's great to be here, Mildred," he said. "You remember Lily, don't you?"

"I surely do," Mildred said. "You're the one who fixed that apple pie with the graham cracker crumbs between the crust and fruit, aren't you? My word, but that was good. You've got to give me that recipe. My man talked about that pie all night."

"Thank you," Lily said. "And I'd be glad to give you the recipe. It was my mother's."

"Great," Mildred said. "I'll give you a call later this evening. I've got company coming tomorrow night. I just might make that pie for dessert."

Case slipped his hand a little farther up her elbow and gave her arm a gentle squeeze as Mildred made an exit across the withering excuse for a lawn.

"Thank you," Lily said quietly and turned to face him.

"For what?" Case asked softly.

"For coming with me. For being there."

His voice was low, but sure. Lily's heart skipped a beat when he answered.

"If you'd let me . . . I'd always be there for you, Lily."

She yanked her arm free and made a dash for her father who was visiting with the preacher beneath the small porch roof.

"Dad! We'd better hurry or I won't have time to get the noon meal."

Morgan nodded, shook the pastor's hand, and then noticed, for the first time, the high color on his daughter's cheeks. He turned around and caught the long, intense look that their host was giving Lily. If he wasn't mistaken, Case had just made a declaration that his girl wanted to ignore.

"We're going to drive into Clinton and eat out," Morgan said. "Case already told us. He said it was your day off."

"But I don't have days off on . . ."

"Obviously you do today," Morgan said. "Come on. Let's get your brothers before they start a riot and we're all run out of town on a rail. I see a couple of nervous fathers already."

Lily tried to ignore Case's existence. But it was hard when he was coming toward her with an expression on his face that brooked no arguments.

"Are you ready?" he asked.

I'll never be ready for you.

Case didn't wait for her answer. He simply guided her back to his truck, and led the way into Clinton for Sunday dinner.

It was late. Lily kept glancing at the clock over the kitchen stove and tried not to be nervous. Case had been gone all evening. By the time it was dark, she'd expected him to come walking into the kitchen at any moment. But he hadn't appeared, and she was beginning to imagine any and every dire emergency befalling him.

One minute they'd been in the den visiting and watching an old movie on television when Duff had come bursting into the house. He shouted something about fences being down and cattle out and Case exited on the run.

Her family's offer to help had been quickly refused. He'd claimed plenty of men were available to do what needed to be done. The Brownfields were to stay and visit with Lily. It was why they'd come. And so they'd visited . . . and finally . . . they'd all retired to their rooms. All but Lily, who waited and worried.

She parted a curtain and stared outside. Nothing but darkness looked back. She quickly dropped it back in place, walked over to the counter, and began rearranging the cutlery drawer for something to do.

Where could they be? Her heart thumped raggedly against her rib cage. Nerves kept her stomach rumbling. *Nothing has happened,* she told herself. *He's just late. No telling what kind of mess they found when they arrived.* But the harder she tried to convince herself she was being silly, the more anxiety developed.

Lily thought about waking her father just to vent her worry and then stopped herself. If she admitted she was worried, then she would have to admit why. It wasn't possible. She couldn't care for this man. The last man she'd cared for had let her down horribly. It hurt too much to face the possibility again.

She slammed the last fork back into place, shuffled the knives although they didn't need shuffling, and then dropped the drawer and its contents onto the floor as the kitchen door suddenly opened.

An entire twelve-place setting of stainless steel cutlery went flying across the shiny linoleum.

As tired as he was, Case began to grin. "Best greeting I've had all day," he said.

"You startled me," she accused, and got down on her hands and knees and began grabbing at the knives, forks and spoons.

"I see that," he said softly, as he knelt to help.

"I can do it," Lily said. "I dropped it . . . I'll clean it up."

"Sometimes, Lily, two sets of hands are better than one. Don't argue with me. I'm too damned tired to hear it."

She swiftly relented as she saw the lines of weariness beneath his eyes and the tired droop to his lips. A thin layer of dust hung over his skin and clothing and his usually bright blue eyes were almost gray with fatigue.

She grabbed his hand and gently took the handful of cutlery from him.

"Go take a bath," she said softly. "I saved some supper for you."

He leaned back on his heels, searching her face for more than concern. He sighed with defeat. It wasn't there.

"I won't be long," he said quietly. And walked away.

Lily knew something more than fatigue was bothering him. She'd felt it ever since church this morning. Sometime between their arrival and their departure, Case had changed. She didn't think it was a religious revelation that had overcome him. But for the life of her, she couldn't quite put her finger on the problem.

If she'd only known to turn around and look in a mirror, Lily Brownfield would have been staring at Case's problem. But if she had, she wouldn't have known how to deal with it. She couldn't even deal with her own.

Case walked back into the kitchen. Tiny droplets of water still beaded across his bare belly where he'd hurried to dry, knowing that Lily was waiting for him. One button was undone at the waistband of his blue jeans and hair was wet and seal black against his neck as he dropped into his seat at the kitchen table.

"Sorry I didn't dress for supper," he said, trying to tease the look of shock off her face. "But as soon as I eat, I'm going to undress again and crawl into bed. Didn't want to waste any time getting there."

Lily tried to ignore all that expanse of bare skin as she filled his plate with food she'd kept warm from the evening meal.

"It doesn't bother me," she said quickly. "I have four brothers, remember?" *But I never wanted to touch my brothers the way I want to touch you.* Her wayward thoughts made her hands shake and she slopped bean juice down the side of the bowl as she carried it to the table.

"Sorry," she said, as she set it down and went to get a cloth. "I kept the cornbread warm but I'm afraid it's going to be a little tough. It just doesn't heat up like other breads. I always think it's a little . . ."

Case grabbed her hand. "Stop it, Lily," he said quietly. "It's fine just the way it is. Don't fuss."

And when he feared that he'd hurt her feelings by being too abrupt, he finished by saying, "I'm not used to having anyone care whether I showed up late or even showed up at all."

"Oh! I wasn't . . ."

Her voice ceased at the look on his face. She couldn't lie, not about that, and not now.

"Well," she said. "I knew you were all right. I just didn't want you to go to bed hungry."

I could eat until morning, and I'd still be hungry . . . for you. "Thank you, Lily. I really appreciate it."

She blushed, and turned to the counter, staring at the jumble of cutlery. "Now I'm going to have to wash this stuff all over again before I put it back," she said.

"I won't tell if you won't," Case said.

Lily turned around and gaped at the innocent look in his eyes. The thought of getting by with something like this was too good to pass.

"Promise?" Her lips twitched with delight at the thought.

"Promise," Case said solemnly. "I never break my word, Lily. That's something you should remember . . . for future reference, of course."

Her hand jerked. She blushed and began sorting the cutlery back into the proper sections. It didn't mean a thing that they were going to share a secret. This was such a silly thing. It didn't mean anything, not anything at all.

She finished, while Case quietly ate. Unaware that every bite he took was followed by a long, contemplative look at her. It was only when she heard his chair scoot back from the table that she realized he was through.

"Well!" she said quickly. "I'll just wash these up and then . . ."

"Leave it," Case said. He set the dirty dishes in the sink, ran them full of water, and turned to face her.

Lily started to argue and then caught the expression in his eyes. She turned her face away and ducked, unconsciously shielding herself from his view.

"Damn it to hell, Lily. I wish you'd stop doing that to me."

She looked up, stunned to see real anger spreading across his face.

"To you? You're not the . . ."

"Yes, I am," he argued. "Everytime I look at you, I'm judged by another man's actions. I don't like it. I don't like it one damned bit."

She started to argue. But it was impossible to argue with the truth. She started to apologize. But it was impossible to talk with her mouth otherwise occupied.

The kiss came suddenly. But somewhere, in the back of her mind, she'd expected it. Maybe that was why she didn't argue. Maybe that was why she didn't move other than to take a step closer.

His arms slid around her, pulling her tightly against bare skin and corded muscles. Her hands moved across his chest and almost slipped up around his neck.

Almost . . . but not quite.

Case sighed as he relinquished his place. He lifted

his head, started to step away, and then gave himself one more taste of Lily.

His lips were warm. The faint taste of hot bread and butter lingered as well as the last cup of coffee he'd consumed. Lily was suddenly hungry all over again but not for food. She shivered as his lips played havoc with her good intentions.

They coaxed and caressed. Firm and possessive, they moved across her face and down the side of her neck, lingering longer at the pulse point below her chin just to savor the knowledge that it raced when he tasted her.

"Case . . ."

He heard the hesitation in her voice. He also heard something else that gave him hope.

"What?" he asked, removing himself from her with supreme effort.

Lily stepped backward in shock. What she'd been about to ask was impossible. She couldn't allow herself to think of such things. But the thought still remained that she'd almost asked him to take her to bed.

"Never mind," she said shortly. "It's late. You'd better get your rest."

Case doubled his hands into fists and resisted the urge to punch a hole in his kitchen wall. He closed his eyes, counted to ten, and when he opened them she was gone.

"Hell," he said quietly. And that's just where his dreams took him later that night.

He tossed and turned, lost in the knowledge that he loved a woman who hated men. Even though he felt her attraction, he knew she was fighting it with every ounce of strength she possessed. That's what frightened him. Lily Brownfield was the strongest woman he'd ever met. He just had to find a way to channel that strength into confidence . . . not distrust.

Lily had felt it. The wanting . . . the need. But it wasn't possible. She'd made her decision a long time ago. No man was worth that kind of pain again. *No man!*

But her dreams took her into a world where a big man's arms held her close. Where the sky and his eyes were one and the same . . . all open . . . all seeing . . . hiding nothing but the truth. Where the heat in her body focused on his touch, and her smile was as clear and smooth as the skin on her face.

And it was only a dream.

SIX

"Buddy, you forgot these," Lily yelled, as she took the stairs down two at a time with a shoe, a belt, and a hairbrush clutched to her breast.

Case came through the front door intent on carrying another load of luggage to the waiting vehicle, but as soon as he saw Lily flying down his staircase he forgot why he'd entered the house. He had an image of how wonderful it would be if he was met in this manner every time he came into his home. He wasn't ready to give up even though Lily ignored every look he sent her way.

Her hair was braided in one thick twist and hung down the middle of her back like a king-size taffy. Her skin was shades browner than the day she'd arrived and made a startling contrast to the natural milk and honey shades of her sun-bleached hair. The yellow, no-nonsense sundress she was wearing added to the image she presented of sunbeams and vitality.

Case caught her as she hit the bottom step on the run.

"Whoa, Lily, love. You'll take a header down those stairs if you're not careful. Take it from one who knows."

Lily turned several shades of red beneath her tan, turned away the side of her face that bore the scar, and wriggled out of his grasp in quick confusion.

She was still heartsick and confused from their late night interlude in the kitchen. She'd been so tempted to allow him what he'd wanted, and so certain that it would be the end of her if she did.

"Stop that," she muttered. "Someone will see. And besides, I'm not your love."

"Not my fault," Case grumbled. "And I don't give a damn if someone does see."

He stalked back outside and left her standing where he'd turned her loose, unaware of the look of longing that followed his exit. Lily couldn't get past the way it had felt to be gathered up in those strong arms and clasped against a cowboy's heart. Los Angeles had not prepared her for a man like Case Longren.

Lily's father and brothers were leaving today and she was nervous, but she couldn't quite put her finger on the reason. At least she'd been unable to until Case Longren had caught her at the bottom of the stairs. Now she knew why she was nervous! She was going to be alone . . . again . . . in this house . . . with Case!

Before her family's arrival she'd been able to keep him at arms' length. Now she'd been in his arms more than she'd been out of them since their arrival. What was going to happen between them after her family left?

"Lilleee! We're leaving!" Buddy yelled.

She moved toward the door on leaden feet. Oh God! Maybe she should just bolt and run. It wasn't too late. She could leave now . . . with her family . . . they'd understand. And Pete could go back to being cook. After all, roundup was nearly over.

The moment Lily came outside clutching Buddy's belongings, Case read the look of panic in her eyes. He wasn't the only one.

"Thanks," Buddy said, as he grabbed his stuff from Lily and tossed it into an already overflowing bag. "What would I do without you?"

It was the perfect opening. Lily started to agree when her father interrupted. He'd seen the look on her face, too, and knew that Cole had been right. Lily needed to see this thing through. She'd already had too many interruptions in her life to allow another. She needed to finish what she'd started.

"That's what's wrong with you, Buddy, my boy," Morgan teased. "We took advantage of Lily much too long and look what we've become! We're nothing but a bunch of moochers. It will be good for us to cope alone again. And, it will be good for Lily to have only herself to worry about. Right, honey?"

His words stopped her intention. Now what could she do? It was patently obvious that she wasn't needed at home after all. Maybe not even wanted. She turned toward Cole and stared, knowing that the bond she had with her oldest brother was the strongest, praying that he'd know what she needed without asking.

Cole pulled her into a roughhouse embrace and whispered softly against her ear as he whirled her around in good-bye.

"You're going to be fine, Lily Kate. Just let whatever your heart tells you to happen, happen. Don't dwell on the past, girl. You've got too much to live for," Cole said.

He put her down, planted a kiss on her surprised mouth, and tugged affectionately at her braid.

"I love you," he said.

"I love you, too, Cole. I love you all," Lily said with tears in her voice. "And I'm so glad you got nosey and came to check on me. I wouldn't have missed J.D. and Dusty's romp with Longren cattle for the world."

Her teasing remarks brought the twins to life as one dug into his pocket and handed her an envelope.

"Here, sis," J.D. said.

"It's for Debbie Randall, your friend from Clinton," Dusty continued.

Lily's eyebrows rose a fraction. She knew that her friend from the grocery store had been at the barbecue and had noticed her brothers had had her in tow more than once during the evening. But she had no idea that their relationship had progressed into letters of good-bye.

"It's not what you think," J.D. grinned. "It's the address of our agent and a letter of introduction for her. She's interested in acting and thinking about making a trip to California. We're just helping her along a bit."

"Not another one," Morgan muttered. "That's not the most encouraging reason to come to California. Half the population of the United States thinks that it's the Mecca for fame and glory."

"Now, Dad," Cole said, "J.D. and Dusty haven't done half bad. Although that's not to say everyone would automatically have their inborn instincts when it comes to telling stories. Hell, they've been lying for years. Now they're getting paid to play make-believe. What's the difference?''

Lily smiled at the banter that ensued as she stuck the envelope into her pocket. Debbie! Acting! She'd never have guessed!

Before she was ready, and before she could think of another reason to prolong their stay, they were heading down the long driveway toward Oklahoma City to catch their morning flight as Lily and Case waved good-bye.

"Are you all right?" Case asked, as he watched Lily swipe at a tear.

"Of course," she said. "Why wouldn't I be? After all, it's not like I'll never see them again. In less than a month roundup will be over and you'll have no more need for a cook on the Bar L.''

Her words hurt. And so did the offhand manner in which they were spoken.

"Well, don't be so damned happy about it," Case growled, and stomped off toward the barns.

Lily's mouth dropped. The morning sun hit her full force as she turned to stare at his retreating figure. Tiny beads of sweat popped out on her upper lip and down the middle of her back. Lily didn't know whether it was from the impending heat, or the sight of his narrow hips and long legs stretching the distance between them. No matter what else she might admit about Case Longren, she couldn't ignore the fact that he was one sexy man.

She lifted her hand to her forehead, shading her eyes as she watched Case walk away. What had prompted that reaction?

A little voice inside her heart told her she already

knew the answer, but she ignored it. What did her heart know about anything? It had steered her wrong once before. It could do it again.

It was Sunday. Everyone's day off. Lily had skipped church and slept in and was now bored. She wished she hadn't been so lazy. She missed the services and the routine and, if she was honest with herself, she missed the people. Lily's Sunday trips to the little country church less than two miles from the ranch had become a habit. She'd been accepted openly. And, it had been good for her heart.

Before her accident, she'd been a people person. She'd always been the first to volunteer to host a party, or help a friend in need. Now she seemed to shy away from too much outside contact for fear of the reaction she imagined people would have at seeing her face. But going to church was easing her back into the public eye.

Lily walked through the downstairs of Case's house, looking absently into each room, knowing that he was somewhere outside and she could roam at will.

She wandered into the den, taking note of the masculine furnishings. The walls of this room were the only ones in the entire house that weren't painted white. Instead, they were paneled in aged, but polished, knotty pine and always made Lily feel comforted when she entered. There was something very homey about wood floors and walls and rock fireplaces.

Her gaze ran along the bookshelves on either side of the fireplace as she toyed with the idea of reading. It didn't appeal. She ran her fingers along the glassed doors of the locked gun cabinet and counted off the number of guns she saw stored inside.

There was even a hunting rifle just like her brother Cole's, and she laughed to herself as she remembered how sore her shoulder had been until she'd learned to shoot it to his satisfaction. She'd actually gotten quite good at target shooting, but hunting left her cold. She couldn't bring herself to kill anything, even an animal that she knew would produce food for her family. She'd rather go to the market and buy something someone else had already dispatched. That way she didn't have to think about how it got there, just how she was going to cook it.

"Miss Lily!"

She jumped as Duff's strident shout broke her reverie. And then the tone of his voice penetrated and she moved out of the den on the run. What was wrong?

"Here," she called, as she ran into the kitchen just as he was heading back outside.

"Oh, thank the Lord," Duff muttered, as he yanked his ten gallon hat from his head and scratched at the sparse grey growth beneath. "I didn't think you was here, Miss Lily."

"What is it?" she asked. And then the blood on his shirt made her gasp. "Are you hurt? There's blood all over your shirt!"

"Ain't mine," Duff muttered. "It's the boss's. He was trying to separate a cow from her calf and she took an instant dislike to the idea."

"No," Lily whispered. "Where is he? How bad is he hurt? Should I call for an ambulance?"

"Lord, no!" Duff cried. "He'd have all our hides. But bring the first aid kit out of the pantry there and come with me. He won't let me see to it and if'n he don't let us clean it up, he could get infected. A barn lot is a prime place for lockjaw. Seen it once m'self.''

Lily yanked open the pantry door and fumbled around in nervous panic until Duff pointed out a case that looked like her father's tackle box. She grabbed it and followed the little foreman out of the kitchen door, praying with every step she took that Case wasn't hurt too badly. If he was, she didn't care how much he argued, he was going to the hospital.

The sun was hanging suspended about halfway between zenith and horizon as Lily ran toward the barn with the tackle box banging against her legs. A stiff breeze had come up just after the noon meal and was stirring the dry, dusty earth with choking precision. Lily breathed in the red dust through her mouth and spit as she ran. She didn't have time to think about the unladylike manner in which she'd done away with the mouthful of dirt she'd inhaled. She was too panicked about Case's blood on the shirt of the little man several strides ahead of her.

"Oh no," Lily muttered, as she rounded the corner of the stable door and stepped into the shade of the entryway.

Case was sitting on a bale of hay just inside the door, mopping at a steady stream of blood that ran out of a long gash down the back of his arm.

He looked up in disgust as he saw his aging foreman and Lily coming toward him with varying degrees of intent on their faces.

"You just had to do it, didn't you," Case growled at Duff. "You just had to go and tell Lily I got a little scratch. What did you think she was going to do? Kiss and make it better?"

"Shut up," Lily said quietly, as she popped the lid of the first aid box and dug through it for some antiseptic and bandage.

Case's jaw dropped. This wasn't exactly the most satisfying bedside manner he'd ever encountered.

"What did you say?" he muttered.

"I said shut up! I'll never understand why men always get mad when they get sick or hurt. My father and brothers are just the same. Duff didn't tell me you needed a kiss, smart aleck, and you're not about to get one. But you're going to get stitches and I'm telling you that for a fact."

Case blanched. Stitches. Damn, damn, damn. And he hated the needles the doctors used to deaden the area a whole lot worse than the actual stitches.

"How did this happen?" Lily asked, as she swabbed carefully through the gash. It was long and, in two places, very, very deep. She thought she could see muscle exposed.

"Cow knocked him against some barbed wire out on the meadow," Pete answered. "Then to add insult to injury, she shoved her head into his belly."

Case mumbled beneath his breath as his ignominious downing was once again bandied about. He hated to be helpless, and he'd been helpless as hell when that cow had had him underfoot.

"Does it hurt to breathe?" Lily asked quickly. He might have some cracked or broken ribs.

"Not so much," Case answered, and then he winced as Lily pulled his arm out to his side and poured a slow, thin stream of alcohol all the way into the cut.

"But that sure as hell does!" he shouted, and yanked his arm away from her ministrations.

"Don't be such a baby," Lily said.

Case took one glance at the look in her eyes, the healed scar on her face, and shut up. He could do no less.

"Now, am I taking you to the hospital, or do you want one of the men to drive you, Case? I'd be glad to, but I'm not familiar with the route and might get us both lost on the way back if they shoot you too full of painkillers."

"I'll take him," Duff said. "Don't move, boss. I'll go get my truck." He scurried in a little two-step motion as he hurried outside toward the bunkhouse.

Case was getting pale, and Lily knew it was probably shock. He'd also lost quite a bit of blood.

"Got any orange juice in the bunkhouse snack bar?" Lily asked. One of the men nodded and ran to get it for her.

Case looked at her as if she'd just asked for bugs.

"When I donate blood, they always give me juice and cookies afterwards," Lily said, answering his question before he had a chance to ask. "I don't think you're up to cookies, but you've lost an awful lot of blood. Maybe the juice will help your nausea."

"How did you know . . ." Case began.

"I've been there, remember?" Lily said.

"Hold this," she ordered, and one of the men obeyed as Lily padded the wound with all the available gauze pads, wrapping them tightly with an ace bandage to hold them in place. The orange juice arrived, and Lily watched the color come back into Case's face as he slowly sipped at the cold drink.

Duff pulled into the stable doorway and yelled out the window.

"Come on, boss. Time's a wastin'."

Case rolled his eyes heavenward, got to his feet, and then staggered as if he'd been punched in the nose. The ground tilted beneath his feet, and he would have fallen if Lily and Pete hadn't grabbed him.

"Hold on to me," Lily said.

Forever, Case thought, as he leaned gratefully against her slender strength and buried his face in the top of her hair. It smelled faintly of cinnamon, and Case knew that he was probably going to miss the apple pies she was baking for supper.

Lily pulled his uninjured arm across her shoulder and wrapped her arm around his waist as Pete propped him up from the other side. Together, they had him in Duff's pickup truck and on the way to the hospital before he had time to argue.

"I'll get that, Miss Lily," Pete argued, as Lily bent down to gather up the bloody gauze she'd dropped on the ground. "You go on up to the house and wash up."

Lily stared down at her blood-stained hands and the spatters of Case's blood on the front of her clothes. She nodded gratefully and started toward the house when one of the men patted her on the back, handed her the first aid box.

"You done real good, Miss Lily," he said. "Real good. Couldn't 'a done better myself. You'd make a real good cowboy . . . I mean cowgirl," he amended with a grin.

"Thanks," Lily said, and walked back to the house with a smile as big as Texas on her face.

She knew that Case would be sore, but unless he had further injuries to his ribs, he'd be healed soon with nothing more than a scar for a reminder.

It was the word scar that brought her up short. Why did it seem so insignificant to her when it was on someone else? Of course, it wasn't on Case's face, but it was still going to be long and ugly and would probably never fade. Was it just possible that everyone viewed her scar in the same manner? Was it possible . . . maybe even true . . . that her scar was of no more importance to others than Case's was to her? *Had* she let Todd Collins's selfish reaction color her own instincts?

Lily walked into the house, replaced the first aid box in the pantry and headed for her bedroom with one purpose in mind.

She walked into her bathroom, turned on the overhead light as well as the light over the vanity and stared. It was still there. But was it as vivid as she'd imagined? Was that the first *and* last thing someone saw when they met, or was it only the first thing? Was Lily, herself, enough to overshadow the disfigurement? Maybe . . . just maybe Case had been telling the truth.

Lily leaned forward until her nose was almost touching the glass and turned first one way and then the other. It still looked as if she was staring into a broken mirror, and the image made her sick. She turned off the vanity light in disgust, turned on the water full force in the sink and proceeded to wash Case's blood from her hands and arms. There was no sense in dreaming about what-ifs. The scar was there, and that was that.

* * *

Supper had come and gone and still no blue pickup truck. Lily sat on the front porch steps, her chin in her hands, and watched the dusky horizon for a glimpse of headlights. It was nearly sundown. She could already hear the crickets tuning up. Several cows were bawling out on the meadow beyond the corrals, obviously searching for the calves that had recently been weaned, and somewhere to the west she could hear dogs barking. Probably chasing a rabbit that hadn't made it back to his hole before nightfall.

Everything was so foreign to the way she'd been brought up, and yet so familiar. Lily knew that if she'd been back in L.A., she would probably be sitting out on her deck, watching the sunset over the ocean and listening to the surf and the night sounds of the city as it came alive in the streets beyond her home.

In L.A. there was always a siren somewhere, and people everywhere. Lily may not have been brought up in the country, but she'd taken to it like icing on a cake. She didn't even want to think about how much she was going to miss all this space and silence when she had to leave. And she absolutely refused to admit that she would miss Case Longren. It didn't bear thinking about.

Lily heard the pickup shift gears as it came around the bend in the road that marked the beginning boundary of the ranch. She breathed a sigh of relief. They were back!

Duff pulled to a stop, but wasn't fast enough to beat Lily to the passenger side of the truck.

"Are you all right?" she asked, as she yanked open the door and peered into the dusky interior.

Duff's cab light was out and all she had to see by was the glare of headlights in front of her. The first thing she saw when she peered inside were blue eyes walled in pain.

Case had never been so glad to see anyone in his whole life. He was hurting like crazy and had been alternating between curses and prayers when Duff turned into the front yard of the Bar L. The little man drove like a bat out of hell and there was no denying it.

"I'm fine," he growled, and stretched one long leg out of the cab, bracing himself on firm ground before swinging the rest of his body out of the cab.

"No, he ain't," Duff argued. "He wouldn't let them doctors give him any more painkillers after they sewed him up and he's sicker than a dog. Doctor said he should have somethin' on his stomach. Might help the nausea. It's caused from all the shots they used to deaden the cut."

"Thank you, Doctor Kildare," Case muttered.

"Help me get him in the house," Lily said. "Then I'll see to the rest."

"I don't need to be carried," Case argued. "Just let me lean on you. I can get myself there."

"Are you sure?" she asked.

"Yes," he answered.

"Then come here, tough boy. I think you've had just about enough for one day." Her words were gentle, but her touch was gentler.

Lily leaned into the cab, offering her shoulder to Case, and stepped to one side as he slid his good arm across her back and swung himself out of the truck.

"Thanks, Duff. See you in the morning."

"Sure thing, boss," the foreman answered, and as soon as Lily and Case had cleared the yard and made their way into the house, he drove back to the bunkhouse and parked, anxious to get inside and regale the men with his version of the boss's trip to the hospital.

Lily maneuvered Case through the front door, up the stairs, and down the hallway to his bedroom without any incident. But as soon as she had him inside his room, he sank down on his bed, not caring about the dust and dried blood on his clothes, and lay back on top of that black satin with no more thought than if it had been a haystack.

"Oh, Case!" she said before she thought. "Your bed!"

"It'll clean," he muttered. "If it doesn't, I'll buy another one. I'm too damn tired to care."

"At least let me take off your boots," Lily argued. She had his foot in hand and the boots off before he had time to disagree.

His shirt had snap fasteners and Lily leaned over and slowly unpopped each one, revealing brown skin and taut muscles. It was sinful to delight in the fact that she could do this without any fear of being misunderstood. He had to have help. It was obvious.

She nudged his shoulder and he grunted as he rolled slightly, allowing her easier access as she slipped his shirt from under him and tossed it to the floor. It was beyond fixing. What the barbed wire hadn't torn, the doctors had cut, to open an area in which to work. A huge dark bruise in varying shades of black and purple was forming on the side and front of his belly, and Lily knew that was a direct result of the blow he'd taken from the cow that had knocked him down. Her fingers drifted gently across the bruise, and then she yanked them back as if she'd been stung. She shouldn't be touching him like that and she knew it.

"How many stitches?" she asked softly, letting her gaze drift across his chest and down the ripple of muscle across his belly.

"A whole damn lot," Case growled, glaring at the long swath of white gauze covering his forearm.

"Could you drink some soup if I brought it up?" Lily asked.

He nodded and watched her walk out of his room with his torn shirt in her hands. He was in fine shape. Here he was in his room, flat on his back in bed with Lily not three steps away, and he couldn't do a damn thing about it. The room swirled around him and he cursed, closed his eyes, and dug his fingers into the satin beneath him, holding on to the only solid thing he could feel. He hated being weak. But even more than that, he hated going to bed in this filthy condition. Not only had he bled all over himself, but he still wore remnants of his roll on the prairie beneath the angry cow's feet.

Case staggered to his feet, wincing every step of the way out of his room and down the end of the hall to the bathroom. By the time Lily made her way back upstairs with a steaming cup of noodle soup, Case had shucked his Levi's, and was taking a shower with his freshly bandaged arm sticking out of the partially opened shower door. He knew enough to not get anything with this many stitches wet. He also knew he was going to have to hurry because he was dizzy as hell and hated to face how he'd look if he passed out buck-naked in the shower. A man had *some* pride.

Lily took one look at the empty room, set the cup of soup down on the bedside table and started out of the door with a look on her face her brothers could have warned Case about.

"Just what do you think you're doing?" she yelled, as she yanked back the bathroom door and saw steam, shower spray, and Case's arm in the midst of it all, pointing shakily toward the ceiling in a weak attempt to keep it dry.

"I'm through." His voice emerged from the clouds of mist and steam, as he turned off the knob to the shower. "Hand me a towel."

"I ought to hand you your head on a platter," Lily grumbled, "but from the looks of you, it probably already feels like it's there."

She handed him a towel, her actions gentler than her tone of voice. And much as she was tempted to do otherwise, she averted her eyes as she helped him from the shower.

"There's nothing worse than a woman who thinks she's always right," Case said as he wrapped the towel around his middle in a halfhearted attempt to conceal his bare rump and masculinity.

"Get yourself in bed, mister," Lily ordered, her green eyes flashing, as she stepped aside and pointed down the hall toward his room.

By the time Case had walked the length of the hall and into his room, his head was spinning, and even though he hated to admit it, his legs felt like a bowl of Pete's cooked-to-death noodles.

Lily pulled back the black satin and a light sheet and blanket that lay beneath, and stood without saying a word as Case sank gratefully into the cool comfort of his own bed. Lily pulled the covers up to his waist before she muttered, ''Hand me that wet towel.''

Case complied weakly as he slid his good arm down beneath the covers and removed his only clothing. He was too shaky to make wisecracks. He'd exceeded his limit by taking a shower, but he'd never been so glad to be clean in his life.

Lily leaned over and grabbed the extra pillow, intent on stuffing it behind his head to prop him up enough to drink his cooling soup, when Case sighed. She could feel his breath against the curve of her neck, and she shivered at the thought of how it would feel to lie naked, skin to skin, with this big man and feel his breath on every square inch of her body.

''My God!'' Lily muttered to herself. This had to stop. ''Can you hold this cup or do you need help?'' she asked sharply, and then regretted her anger the moment it came out. Case didn't deserve to suffer just because she was having some kind of sexy hot flash.

Case stared. Her words were sharp, but the expression on her face and the gentleness of her touch told him that she cared.

''I can manage,'' he said quietly, and took the cup from her hands and drained it. ''Thanks, Lily Catherine,'' he said. ''You'd make a very good nurse, if you'd just work on your bedside manner a bit.''

Lily started to argue when she saw the look in his eyes. Even in pain he was trying to make her smile. She felt a sharp tug in the region of her heart and knew that it was her conscience telling her to put up or shut up. She opted for the latter.

Lily took the empty cup, set it down and pulled the extra pillow out from under his head. She couldn't resist swiping at the dark, black swath of hair that kept trying to slide across his forehead and she brushed at it gently as she tested his forehead for signs of a fever.

"Where are your pain pills?" Lily asked.

"Probably in my pants pocket," Case mumbled, already nearly asleep. "But I'm not taking any of the damn things. They give me a hell of a hangover. Got too much to do tomorrow."

Lily ignored his arguing, hurried to the bathroom, retrieved the jeans and found the bottle of pain relievers in his front pocket. But by the time she returned to his room, Case was fast asleep. She set them down on his bedside table, filled a glass with water and set it beside the pills. She started to leave the room but then turned for one last look.

He looked so hurt and lonely, his bandaged arm flung out and away from the rest of his body, and she resisted the urge to crawl in beside him and just hold him tightly against her heart all through the night. She could remember vividly the pain of awakening in the dark, hurting and alone, and couldn't face the thought of Case suffering the same way.

Before she could talk herself out of it, she'd dashed downstairs, slipped into her pajamas and a housecoat, grabbed a blanket and pillow, and headed back upstairs to Case's room. If he awoke in the night in pain, she'd be there.

Lily couldn't face the reason why she'd done something this foolish as she curled herself into a ball on the floor across from his bed and pulled the blanket around her. She didn't want to hear the voice inside her heart telling her that she'd just stepped over a line in their relationship. She wasn't listening to anything but the restless sleep of the big man in the bed.

SEVEN

Case watched out of the corner of his eye, feigning sleep as Lily raised her head from the pillow, looked toward his bed, then quietly dragged herself to a standing position, gathered her blanket and pillow into a careless wad and staggered out of his room. It was almost dawn.

A lump formed in the back of his throat and he blinked rapidly, willing away the emotion that swept over him at the knowledge that Lily had slept on the floor in his room just to make certain that he came to no harm during the night.

He rolled over on his back, wincing as his heavily bandaged arm came in contact with the bedcovers, took a deep breath, swallowing what felt suspiciously like a sob, and ran his good hand over his face, feeling the heavy growth of his stubbly whiskers pricking the palm of his hand. He stared at the pattern of shadows forming on the ceiling overhead from the first hint of morning and knew he could deny his true feelings for Lily no longer.

He'd long ago admitted to himself that he loved her. He'd tried over and over during the last few weeks to let Lily know that his feelings for her were special, but it wasn't until this moment, when he'd watched her sleep, that he'd known the depth of his own emotions.

If Lily Brownfield left him, he would not survive.

For the first time, he had an inkling of the pit his father had fallen into when his mother had abandoned them. Now he knew what had made Chock Longren go to hell in a bottle. It was for something more than love. It was an enduring need to be near and to care for someone other than himself. To lose all selfish desires of pleasure for himself, and have only the desire to please another. There was no name in Case's vocabulary for the need he had to lie next to Lily and simply watch her sleep. To know that he had the right to hold her, fight for her, comfort and care for her for the rest of his days as they grew old together.

A slow, aching moan slipped out from between his tightly clenched lips and he covered his eyes and cursed. He had to do something to knock down the wall of hurt behind which Lily lived. He'd do anything it took to keep her here on the Bar L with him when roundup was over. He couldn't lose her.

Lily had awakened during the night to hear Case mumbling in his sleep. She knew he was hurting. She could tell from the way he kept rolling over and then back as he'd accidentally bump or bend his injured arm. And she suspected that the bruising on his side and belly were contributing to the discomfort he seemed to be suffering.

She got up from her pallet on the floor, tiptoed to his bed, shook two of the pain pills from the bottle, slid her arm beneath his head and whispered softly in his ear, rousing him just enough to get him to swallow.

"Case, open your mouth, sweetheart," she whispered, using the endearment without thought.

He obeyed without opening his eyes. Lily slipped the tiny pills into his mouth, grabbed the glass of water from his bedside table, pressed it to his lips and gently tilted it.

"Take a sip," she urged. "It's only water. It'll help you sleep."

Lily tipped the glass as Case drank thirstily, unknowingly swallowing the pills along with the water he was gulping greedily. She set the glass back on the table, slipped her arm out from beneath his head, letting it fall gently back onto his pillow.

"Get some sleep," she whispered against his ear and then she ran her fingertip beneath his lower lip, catching the tiny drip of water that lingered and wondered at the ache in her heart as she resisted the urge to taste the moisture where it lay.

He turned and murmured against the palm of her hand and Lily knew that by morning, he would remember none of this. It was just as well.

She straightened his covers, letting her eyes gaze greedily on his bare chest and broad shoulders. Even in the darkness they were visible against the ivory sheen of the bedclothes.

Something was happening to her. Lily knew it. She'd stopped trying to deny it. She was slowly but surely falling in love with Case Longren, and it could only end in disaster for her.

She had thought that she loved Todd. But the feelings she'd had when she'd been with him were nothing to the curl in the pit of her stomach that appeared whenever she saw Case. He made her hot and cold all over . . . all at the same time . . . always.

She had only to look up into that face, look at the strong ruggedness of his features, the thick, jet black hair that lay across his forehead in a constant state of windblown abandon, and those eyes . . . pieces of the wide Oklahoma sky piercing into her soul, and she wanted to lie down beside him and never get up. If only she'd met Case Longren first. If only he'd been the man she was engaged to when she'd had her accident. If only . . . Lily sighed. If-onlies were for dreamers, and she didn't believe in dreams anymore.

She tiptoed back to her makeshift pallet, wrapped herself in the blanket and curled into a ball of misery, waiting for morning to come.

She was still awake when the first hint of dawn slipped between the sheer curtains hanging from the window in Case's room. Swallowing repeatedly at the huge lump that hung in the back of her throat, she allowed herself one last look at Case before she crept from the room. It would have to be enough to last her. She didn't dare risk having him wake up. He would have had her in bed before she could say maybe.

Lily's shower was swift, her toilet haphazard, as she pulled her swath of hair back away from her face, twisting it into a loose knot at the nape of her neck and fastening it with a couple of long, decorative hair combs. She grabbed a fresh shirt from a hanger—its mint green stripes a cool, crisp addition to her no-nonsense hairdo—a clean pair of Levi's, and a pair of canvas deck shoes and dressed in a hurry. She wanted to fix Case some breakfast and take it up before the men arrived for their morning meal. It wouldn't be out of the ordinary for someone to have a meal in bed after a day like Case had had.

At least that's what she kept telling herself as she carried the steaming tray of food all the way up the stairs and into his room.

"It's about time you woke up," she said cheerfully as she peeked into the half-open door and saw Case sitting up in bed, poking at his ribs as if testing his stomach muscles for soreness.

Case looked up in surprise to see Lily carrying a tray toward him. He hadn't expected to see her so soon, and he certainly hadn't expected to see her smiling.

"What's this?" he asked suspiciously.

"Breakfast," she answered, ignoring the look of shock on his face. She knew men. They were all alike. Tough as nails when it suited them, and babies one and all when they were sick or hurt.

"In bed?"

His voice rose somewhere between one and two octaves and he looked around, halfway expecting to see Duff poke his head through the doorway and laugh at him. Real men didn't eat breakfast in bed! At least none of the men Case had ever known.

He didn't know whether to be happy about the fact that he didn't have to get up and maneuver down the stairs in front of all the men, or be embarrassed by the fact that Lily was here with his food.

"Smooth down your covers," she ordered, and carefully placed the tray down on his lap after he'd hurried to do her bidding.

"Now, do you need anything else?" she asked, letting her eyes feast on the sight of Case, with his sleep-ruffled hair, bedroom eyes gazing at her from under heavy lids, and the long, long length of him hidden beneath the covers over his feet and legs.

Case grinned and picked up his fork, sniffing appreciatively at the array of food in front of him.

"Do you really expect me to answer that?" he teased, running an appreciative look slowly up and down her slender body.

Lily blushed and made a quick pivot as she darted for the door. "Well, you're certainly feeling better this morning," she grumbled. "If you're back to hinting at stuff like that, you're just fine."

"Where are you going, Lily love," Case yelled. "Aren't you going to feed me?"

"You can't possibly want me to put that food where I'm thinking, mister," Lily muttered, as she made a beeline out the doorway.

His laughter followed her down the hall, down the stairs, and all the rest of the day inside her heart.

The week passed in a flurry of renewed activity. Case had supervised the rest of the week's work from the sidelines, careful not to get his stitches torn or dirty. He had no intention of undoing the work the doctor had done and go through a repeat of his trip to the hospital. Tough he may be, but needles he hated.

Lily dodged most of his attempts to get her alone, and then she suffered in silence when he would eventually give up, unaware that she watched him walk away with his name on her lips.

On Saturday, it was time for Lily's weekly trip to town. Case had gone to the hospital to get his stitches removed and although the day had continually threatened rain, she decided to make the trip alone. She'd been so many times since her arrival that the store manager had begun calling her by her first name every time she walked into the store.

She'd taken the time to linger and have lunch with Debbie but had finally been persuaded to hurry home after they'd come out of the restaurant and Debbie had taken a good long look at the dark sky overhead.

"It looks bad," Debbie cautioned.

Lily glanced upward, looking at the dark, almost green cast the heavy, low-hanging clouds wore, and shrugged.

"It's not raining," she argued. "And besides, what's a little rain? Shoot, Debbie. There's not even much wind."

"That's just the point," Debbie said. "It looks like twister weather."

"Twister? What kind of weather is that?" Lily asked.

"It's weather from hell," Debbie answered. "Take it from me, girl. You get yourself in that station wagon and you head for home now. And Lily . . ."

"What?" Lily answered. Debbie's behavior was beginning to sink in as Lily realized that she was truly concerned about her being out on the road.

"Call me when you get home. I want to know that you arrived safely," Debbie begged.

"Sure thing," she muttered, as she cast a nervous glance upward. The drive home had been nerve wracking. She'd spent half the time looking at the road in front of her and the other half casting worried glances up toward the dark, boiling clouds. In spite of Debbie's warnings of doom and gloom, she'd arrived safely at the Bar L, unloaded her groceries, and was safely inside before the first drops of rain fell. She made the promised call to Debbie, assured her that she was safe and sound, and then began unpacking the mountain of food she'd just purchased for the men.

Several times she walked toward the kitchen window, staring at the rain and wind and the dark, low-hanging clouds.

At Case's insistence, she didn't cook that evening. Instead, she set out sandwich stuffs and snack type foods for the evening meal, since the men had ceased work before noon due to the weather. Case had fixed himself a sandwich but refused to seat himself at the table with the men. He'd carried the snack outside and ate it while standing on the porch, searching the overhung clouds between bites.

Due to the downpour, the men had driven rather than walked up to the main house for their meal. They had finished in record time and made a dash back outside for their vehicles, anxious to get inside the bunkhouse and settle down for a lazy, early night.

Lily stared at them as they scattered through the rain like quail running for cover. She quickly put the kitchen back in order and wandered through the living room and den, pretending to check all the windows to make sure they were closed against the rain; in fact, she was searching for Case. She finally located him in the den, perched on the edge of his favorite easy chair, seemingly transfixed by the show that was playing on the television. If something was that interesting, it deserved his entire attention, she thought, and sighed, leaving him to watch his show in private.

But Case wasn't paying attention to the sitcom that he'd tuned into. He was reading the line of script that kept running beneath the picture, mentally taking note of the direction the thunderstorm was moving as the weatherman's warning continually ran across the bottom of the screen. He hated stormy weather, especially when there were tornado warnings. He'd been in one tornado. One was enough!

All evening and late into the night he kept going from the television to the porch outside, scanning the dark, searching the skies. In the instant when lightning would illuminate the heavens, he'd have a chance to look for telltale signs of a deadly tail of twisting cloud hanging down from the sky.

He knew the hour that Lily had given up on him and gone to bed. She'd stuck her head inside the doorway and told him goodnight. But for once, Case had not been tempted to tease her or follow her down the hall and take a chance on sneaking a goodnight kiss. He'd been too concerned about their welfare.

Because he'd been so uncommunicative, he knew Lily probably thought he was angry. In fact, it had been just the opposite. He had no intention of telling her what was bothering him. He didn't want to frighten her unnecessarily. Many times, nights like this resulted in nothing but sleeplessness. The storms usually blew over. But it was the one time that it didn't that had to count. It was too dangerous to just go to bed and hope that when morning came you were still alive to wake up.

Lily had been asleep for what seemed like hours. The constant drumming of rain overhead lulled her into a deep, dreamless sleep that was broken by a clap of thunder so loud that she felt the bed actually shake from the shockwaves.

Following that, Case's harsh, urgent voice was in her ear, and the feel of his strong arms scooping her from the bed, blankets and all, made Lily think she was dreaming. But she'd never felt such fear in her sleep. And when Case kicked open the back door and made a run off the porch into the blinding rain, soaking them both to the bone, Lily knew this wasn't a dream. It was a nightmare!

"Stand up!" Case shouted into her ear, desperate to be heard over the pounding rain and the continuous rumbling growl of thunder overhead. "I've got to open the cellar door."

When Lily's feet touched the ground, she felt water come over her ankles. He'd either put her in a puddle, or else he was trying to drown her. She didn't know which and was too frightened and cold to care. The wind whipped at the blanket that Case had wrapped around her, and she clutched at it in panic, afraid that if it blew away into the night, she'd go with it.

"Case!" she screamed, as the wind tore at her hair and clothing, suddenly realizing that she could no longer see or feel him anywhere near.

Instantly he was there, wrapping his arms around her shoulders as a faint beam of light from the flashlight in his hands shined a weak but welcome path down the cellar steps.

"Come on, honey," he yelled above the storm, "just get inside. We'll be okay. I promise!"

Lily didn't wait for a second invitation. She all but jumped down the steps, unaware of what she was walking into, yet knowing that it could be nothing as frightening as what they'd just left.

"Are you all right, Lily Catherine?" he asked, as she jumped at the sound of rocks hammering on the cellar door.

"What's that?" she asked, unable to mask a shiver of fright. She pulled the damp blanket closer around herself.

"Hail," Case answered grimly. And they sounded big. Their impact was echoing inside the cellar like a drumbeat gone wild.

Case laid the flashlight on a shelf, letting the little beam of spotlight shine toward Lily's face as his hands ran swiftly up and down her shaking arms, searching for signs of injury.

He'd all but dragged her from her bed and wasn't sure whether he'd carried her as carefully as he'd liked. He hadn't had time to be a gentleman about the dash to the storm cellar.

He'd fallen asleep in front of the television and awakened to a weatherman beeping a tornado warning for their vicinity. It had taken him exactly one second to realize that they might not have time to get to a cellar before he'd discarded the notion and headed for Lily's room on the run. He had to get her to safety.

"Answer me, Lily. Are you all right?" he asked anxiously.

Lily nodded her head and blinked, suddenly blinded by the light. She shuddered as she felt Case's hands on her body.

Case felt her tremble and hauled her against him before she had time to argue.

"I'm sorry, Lily love. So sorry," he crooned, as he wrapped his arms around her shoulders and pressed her wet, shaking body against the strength of his own. "I didn't mean to scare you to death, but there almost wasn't time to get here. I fell asleep in the chair. I didn't hear the warning."

"Warning?" Lily muttered. The moisture on his bare chest began to warm from the body heat and started to run down onto her face. "What warning?"

She tried to remember what he'd been saying, but the feel of being soaking wet and plastered to Case was a powerful aphrodisiac.

"Tornado warning," he answered, and then a deep, overwhelming shudder swept over him. Lily's tongue snaked out against his chest and licked at the remnants of raindrops clinging to his body.

"What the hell are you doing?" he growled, as he swelled instantly beneath the zipper of his equally wet Levi's.

He tangled his hands in the wet fall of her hair, tilting her head until he could see directly into her eyes. Wide, wild, and green, they stared back at him in aching confusion.

"Lily?" The question was a caution and a prayer, all at the same time.

Lily turned her head, looked over her shoulder at the ancient iron bedstead and the pillow-ticking mattress taunting her from the shadows of the roomy cellar and then back up at Case's face. She leaned back, moving away from his hold just enough to allow breathing room.

It was a mistake.

Her nightgown was soaking wet, and after being plastered against Case, was clinging to her body like wet tissue paper. Every lush curve and dark valley of Lily's body was there for Case to see. She gasped and started to pull the blanket back up around her in embarrassment when a harsh grunt from Case and the touch of his hand made her stop.

He felt like he had the day the cow had butted him in the stomach. Only this time it was Lily who had him down and helpless. He was hard and aching and to the point of insanity just from looking at the beauty of Lily beneath the wet gown.

Lily saw his hand suspended between the space separating them, unmoving . . . waiting for a sign . . . uncertain which way this night would go. She made the decision for them both. It was the only thing she could do.

She stepped forward, letting his hand fall against her breast, and laid her head against his heartbeat.

"Oh God!" Case muttered. "Lily, do you know what you're doing? In about three seconds, I'm not going to be able to think."

"Don't think," she whispered, as she leaned sideways and flipped off the flashlight. "Just feel!"

Her whispered command was not lost on Case as he swept her into his arms and in one long stride, had her on her back, on the bed, and beneath his wet, throbbing body.

"Lily . . . Lily . . . Lily," he whispered, maddened by the feel of her softness, aching from the need to bury himself in her warmth. "Touch me, love. Help me love you."

Lily's hands slipped out from between them as she dug her fingers into the taut band of muscles across his shoulders and arched her lower body into him, desperate to ease the ache between her legs that was driving sanity out into the night with the storm.

Thunder rumbled and the wind sucked through the air vent of the cellar overhead as Lily gave her heart to the man above her. Tonight, no matter what the cost, no matter how wrong, she would not deny this wild need she had to belong to him. If only for a moment, if only for a night, she would have Case Longren as no one ever had. She would make him forget that she was less than perfect to look at. She would be the perfect lover for the perfect man.

Case buried his face in the valley between her breasts and moaned, trying to maintain a level of civilized behavior when all he wanted to do was lose himself in the tempting woman moving in a slow taunt beneath him. He heard her moan, and felt her sigh as she moved her legs just enough to allow him space between them, and then he was lost.

Case grasped the neck of her nightgown, intending to pull it upward and off, when Lily slid her hand off his shoulder and down past his waist into the narrow space between their hips. Her fingers splayed across him, feeling his ache as vividly as if it were her own, and the moan that came up her throat was his undoing.

His hand tightened at the neck of the garment, its fragile fabric weak and pliant from the rain. He yanked downward, splitting it asunder by the lightning quick motion. Lily's breasts came free beneath his chest.

"Case," Lily whispered, "make love to me. Love me, if only for tonight, love me."

"Not just tonight," he groaned, as his mouth found the aching bud of her breast. "Forever."

She was sweet, and warm, and wet, and she was driving Case wild. Her hands touched, her body moved, and her mouth pleaded and tasted until he was uncertain whether he'd actually made it to the cellar after all. He felt himself lifted and he felt himself fall. She was as wild and unchained as the storm above them, and Case knew that the waiting was almost over.

Lily's body was humming beneath his fingers, the blood racing through her veins as the madness he'd started overtook and then swallowed her whole. She tried more than once to speak, beg for an end to the exquisite torture of lying beneath Case's body, but each time she'd opened her mouth, it had taken all of her breath just to get past the touch of his mouth and hands and the wicked magic he was working on her heart.

When he'd moved away only long enough to peel off his wet jeans, Lily had been stunned by the loss she'd experienced. In the instant it had taken for him to slide back upon her body, she'd been overwhelmed by the feeling of homecoming she experienced when he'd wrapped her in his arms and claimed her with a kiss that shook her soul. Nothing in her life had prepared her for Case.

His body was hard, his manhood a constant throbbing ache. Case shuddered, and Lily responded with one silky movement that slipped him down and in place so smoothly he nearly lost control right then and there. And the whisper Lily sent across his mouth finished him. Now there would be no turning back.

"I'm on fire, Case," Lily begged, as she moved beneath him. "Everything hurts."

"Not for long, love," he promised, and nearly lifted Lily from the bed as he took positive possession of his L.A. woman.

The motion was fluid, the movement unbearable because for a heartbeat he stayed motionless, allowing her body to adjust to his presence. Lily began to shake, suddenly aware of how far she'd gone, and the distance yet to go, and began to cry from the joy, softly at first and then frantically as Case slowly moved within her.

Everything came too fast and then not fast enough. His body taught, his body teased, and then his body took her up and over the whirling maelstrom of the storm outside and into a storm of their own that left them both shaking and weak, lost in the quiet aftermath of passion's tempest.

Soft whispered words of love, endearments so special Lily knew that she'd die before she ever heard anything so sweet again, and gentle caresses so tender it brought tears to her eyes were coming from Case to Lily with love.

She buried her face in his shoulder, digging her nails into his back in an effort to deny what had to happen next. Soon she would have to get up and face him, knowing that what he'd held in the darkness would be less in the light.

Lily had no doubt that Case loved her. What had just transpired between them could not have resulted solely from lust. But it *had* been in the dark. Lily couldn't bring herself to believe that he would have worshipped her or her body as well had there been light by which to make love. How could he make love with so much beauty to one so ugly? Lily was convinced she was right. She had to be. Distance and distrust were her only protection against the pain of rejection.

The wind was dying down, the hail had ceased, and it sounded as if the rain had lessened. Case leaned forward, cupped Lily's face in the darkness as surely as if there were light all around them, and ran his tongue down the thin line of scar across her cheek, letting it slide the full length of the healed cut before slipping it sideways and into her mouth, relishing the shocked "O" her lips made at his audacious action. He made one swift survey of the tasty sweetness of her mouth before withdrawing with a sigh of regret.

"Sounds like the worst of the storm has passed. I'd better get dressed and check. There may not be a house to go back to, love."

"Oh no!" Lily gasped, as she felt around in the darkness for the remnants of her nightgown. She hadn't envisioned the possible consequences of such a storm.

"It wouldn't matter," Case said quietly, as he stepped into his Levi's and boots and then felt around for the flashlight he'd left on the shelf. "I have you. That's the only thing I don't want to lose. Everything else can be replaced but you, my Lily, and don't you ever forget it."

Case switched on the light, turned it toward the

bed and Lily, and watched the startled expression she wore change into one of quiet acceptance.

She dropped the edge of nightgown she'd started to pull over herself to hide her nudity, and instead, propped herself on one elbow and lay silently beneath the glow of the flashlight as a woman who knows her man. She started to turn away that most hated side of her face when the look she saw in Case's eyes stopped her thought. Instead she tilted her head back, letting her honeyed tangle of hair fall across her shoulders and back down onto the bed, daring him to stare at the imperfection.

Case's hands shook as he held the flashlight, and knew an instant of desire so strong it was as if they'd never made love. He started to unsnap the Levi's he'd just fastened and crawl back into the bed beside her when Duff's anxious voice and the thump of his boots on the cellar door startled them both. It sent Lily grabbing for her torn nightgown and the wet blanket on the cellar floor.

He helped her cover herself until no one could tell that she'd just been sweetly ravished, placing one last kiss at the worry on her face. He stepped between Lily and the doorway just as Duff yanked back the door, and he shielded her from sight as he answered Duff's anxious plea.

"We're just fine," he said, as he saw Duff peer down into the shadowy depths of the cellar. "Everyone else okay?"

"Yep," Duff answered, "we went into the old barn. Not a scratch on a soul."

Case knew that the men always took shelter in one of his dad's older outbuildings. The lower level of the barn had been built into the side of a hill and served as an emergency shelter from these storms.

"We're fine, boss," Duff repeated. "But I ain't so sure about the stable roof. Grab your light and come with me. The rain's about over and I got the men out checking on stuff now."

"Be right there," Case answered. "I just want to make sure Lily is safely inside the house first."

"Sure thing," Duff answered, and left the cellar door open as he hurried away into the night.

Case started to turn around when Lily's arms came from behind his back and wrapped around his waist. He felt her head against the middle of his back as she whispered softly into the shadows surrounding them.

"I wish this storm had never passed," she said sadly.

Case turned in her arms and tilted her head up to face him.

Lily stared into blue so hot and wild she started to shake.

"Honey, it's just started," he promised, as he bent down and took the breath right out of her body with a kiss that sealed the pledge of his words.

EIGHT

"Sleep," Case had ordered, after bringing her back into the house and carrying her safely over the blanket of hail that the storm had left as a reminder of its passing.

And she had . . . like the dead. Lily never even knew when Case returned from checking storm damage with Duff. She'd abandoned the torn nightgown where it had fallen, shakily pulled on some old, comfortable sweats, and crawled back between the covers.

Next to the last thing she remembered before falling asleep was that she was glad she'd kept taking birth control, because tonight she'd completely lost control. And the last thing she remembered before her eyes closed was how she'd felt when Case had taken total possession of her body . . . replete . . . and complete. It was something wonderful on which to dream.

Much later, the smell of freshly brewed coffee

drifted down the hallway and into Lily's bedroom. She wrinkled her nose, turned over on her back and sleepily opened one eye just to see if she was dreaming. Sunlight stared her straight in the face, and Lily nearly fell out of bed, shocked by the sight of so much day.

"Oh no!" Lily moaned, as she glanced at the digital clock on her bedside table. Its little red numbers flashing over and over like a neon sign told her that sometime in the night the power had gone off and her alarm had failed to ring.

She made a run for the bathroom, and less than a minute later was out of her room and down the hall, still dressed in the sweats she'd slept in, heading for the kitchen with her hair flying and shoes in hand.

She didn't know what she'd expected to see, but it wasn't Case standing barefoot, wearing jeans and a blue western shirt that was unsnapped and untucked. The men were nowhere in sight. There was no one but Case, nursing a cup of coffee and staring out of the kitchen window with a frown on his face.

"I overslept," she mumbled, as he swerved around at her entrance.

"I know," he said softly, set his coffee down and came toward her, his bare feet making tiny pat-pat sounds on the red-tiled floor.

Lily didn't know how to act. She'd never had to face "morning afters" before. She needn't have worried. Case's smile swept over her from head to toe just as he gathered her into his arms and pulled her off her feet.

"Good morning, Lily Catherine," he whispered.

He bent down and kissed her flushed cheeks, one after the other, and then moved to the tempting sweetness of her mouth, savoring the lingering remnants of her peppermint mouthwash.

Lily had never before had morning coffee in quite so desirable a fashion. But the taste of it on Case's mouth as he nipped at the bottom of her lip sent a jolt of adrenaline into her system that no amount of caffeine could have ever duplicated.

Lily was torn between reciprocating and retreating. She didn't know whether to let what had happened last night be the beginning or the end. She knew what she wanted, she just didn't know if it was wise. She'd been hurt too badly before to trust her heart this quickly again.

The moment they'd kissed, Case felt her withdrawal. A knot of anger clutched in the pit of his stomach. He set her back down on her feet and released his hold on her shoulders, piercing her guilty stare with icy shards of blue fire.

"Don't do this, Lily," he growled. "Not after last night. You can't send a man to heaven with one hand and yank him to hell with the other."

His words hurt, but Lily knew he was justified. She remained silent and watched him turn away from her in disgust.

"I'll be out most of the day," he muttered, as he turned around, unwilling for her to see the pain on his face. "Just keep a pot of stew or beans on the stove. Nothing fancy. The men will come to eat in shifts. We'll be cleaning up most of the day."

The storm! Lily was shocked that she'd just remembered. So much had happened between them last night that she'd nearly forgotten the fierce winds and the rain and hail.

"Was there much damage?" she asked.

"Damage?" He shoved his hand angrily through his hair, shoving its inky black, shower-damp style completely out of order. "Hell, yes, there was damage! All kinds of things were torn up last night. All kinds of things."

He left her with a hard stare and the cryptic remark that Lily suspected had nothing at all to do with the damage resulting from the storm. She knew Case was referring to what had happened between them. And, with her reluctance to commit herself to a relationship, she'd just torn the first fragile bonds of trust that had been forming. In spite of her fears and her need to protect herself, she wasn't so certain that it had been the right thing to do.

She heard Case go up the stairs and before long, come back down again, this time booted and ready. Lily started through the kitchen toward the front of the house, intent on catching him—for what reason, she hadn't decided—but it was too late. She got nothing but a backside view of his ramrod straight shoulders as he slapped his black Stetson on his head and slammed the door shut behind him.

Lily pressed shaky fingers to her lips, intent on stopping their tremble, but it was no use. Tears squeezed past her lashes anyway, running in guilty tracks down the sides of her face. She pressed her palms against her cheeks, bitterly swiping at the tears of regret and made her way back toward her room. She had to get dressed and get busy. It was going to be a long day.

Noon had come and gone and the day was growing warmer by the minute. She couldn't believe that the night before it had been cold enough to rain baseball-size chunks of frozen ice; less than twelve hours later it was warm enough for short sleeves. Oklahoma weather was one for the books.

Lily screwed the lid down on the large thermos she'd filled with iced tea, grabbed a big sack of freshly baked oatmeal cookies and started out the back door of the house. The farther she walked away from the house, the more evidence she saw of the storm's devastating aftermath.

She knew that they'd been lucky in one respect. There *had* been a tornado. That much had been confirmed by several of the men who'd seen it coming across the prairie, but at the last minute its tail had pulled back up into the clouds and passed over the ranch house with a checkerboard hop. It was the strong side winds and the hail that had done the most damage.

Anywhere Lily looked she could see missing shingles, panels of tin from the barn roof wrapped around fence posts, and broken tree branches and leaves. Several of the windows on one side of the house had been cracked or broken. Duff's blue pickup truck had a windshield shattered from blowing debris, and a long section of fence was down along the driveway. A wall from a small outbuilding had blown across it and been dragged far enough that it had snapped the top two strands of barbed wire.

Men were everywhere. For the moment, roundup was forgotten as they tried to put the Bar L back into working order.

Lily walked toward the barns where the largest number of men were working. Duff was the first one to see her coming and waved a hello and a happy grin as he spied her carrying refreshments.

"I hope it's wet and I hope it's cold," he said, as Lily handed him the thermos and a handful of paper cups.

Pete dug into the sack, grabbed a couple of the spicy cookies for himself and then passed the bag around as the men gratefully took a break and poured themselves a cup of the iced tea to go with their snack.

"Where's Case?" Lily finally asked. She suspected that he was purposefully ignoring her.

Duff frowned and swiped at his mouth with the back of his hand, removing cookie crumbs and tea droplets in one fell swoop.

"Aww, he's out back, burying calves," he answered. "Damn shame, too."

For a moment, Lily couldn't speak. She was dumbfounded. Burying calves? Surely the winds hadn't been that strong? How did storms such as the one last night cause animals to die? This was all out of her realm of expertise.

Lily walked around behind the barn and headed for a small rise where she saw Case climbing down from a tractor. The closer she came to Case, the faster she walked, until she was almost running. She met him coming around behind the piece of equipment.

The look on his face stopped whatever question she'd been about to utter. He stared at Lily with a look of surprise on his face, traces of drying tears on his cheeks still there for her to see.

She didn't know what had happened, and she didn't know what Case had been doing, but she knew what he needed. She opened her arms, and he walked into them like a lost child who's just found the front door to home.

"Damn hail," he muttered, as he dug his fists into the wild, honeyed tangle of her hair and buried his face in its sweetness.

She smelled of lemon and soap, cinnamon and spice, and he'd never felt so complete in his entire life.

"Hail?" Lily didn't follow his line of thought. But it didn't matter, just holding Case was enough for now.

"Yeah," he said, as he rested his chin on the top of her head and pulled her nose into the dip between his collar bone, letting his hands roam at will up and down her back as he stared sightlessly across the rolling hills of his ranch. "Hail was too big and some of the calves were too small. Got caught out in the open. I had to bury four. Damn shame, too," he muttered. "They were so little."

Lily caught her breath, knowing that another side of the man she'd come to love had just been revealed to her. He was a man of the land. He not only raised the animals, but cared for them in the true manner of a shepherd watching over his flock. And when one was lost, he grieved for it because he'd failed in his duty to care and protect.

"I'm so sorry, honey," she said, not realizing that she'd used an endearment.

Case didn't intend to remind her of her slip. He was too busy holding on for dear life. He was sorry as hell that he'd just lost four of his best calves, but he'd lose the whole damn herd if that's what it took to keep Lily Brownfield in his arms forever.

Lily hugged him gently and then stepped away,

suddenly aware of how open and exposed they were, standing in each other's arms in plain sight of the ranch.

"Are you finished here?" she asked. "I brought some iced tea and cookies to the men. If you hurry, there might be a few left."

"Hop on," Case ordered, as he vaulted into the seat of the tractor and held out his hand for Lily to climb up beside him.

"Oh no!" she muttered, backing away from the big, green machine with an apprehensive look on her face. "I'll just walk."

"Scared?" Case asked, still holding out his hand.

Lily stared. First at the machine, then at the distance back to the barns, then back at the tractor, and up at Case's face. It was the latter that swayed her decision. There was more than just trust in his driving ability at stake here. It was a matter of trust in Case, the man.

"I'm not scared with you," she answered, and reached up, feeling the strong grip of his fingers wrap around her wrist and pull until she was sitting beside him in the tractor seat, her arms wrapped around his neck to keep from falling.

Her answer would be enough to get him through the rest of the day. With Lily he knew he'd have to take one step at a time. One very *small* step, at a time. *Hell's fire, I'd crawl*, he thought, *if that's what it takes, I'll crawl. But I will have Lily. I have no other alternative*.

They'd no more than parked the tractor beside the barn when a truck came down the driveway and pulled to a stop in front of the area where the men were working. A big, heavyset man with bulging muscles and a matching stomach that hung heavily over his pants slid out of the truck. He sauntered over to Case who was helping Lily down from the high tractor seat.

The smile she gave Case went a long way toward healing the hurt she'd dealt him earlier this morning. If he was patient, surely she'd know that she was more than just a pretty face to him. He almost forgot that the trucker had arrived until he spoke. Case turned at his announcement.

"Got your load of sheet metal and two by fours," the man said, pointing back over his shoulder with his thumb as he shifted a toothpick from one side of his mouth to the other with his tongue. "Where ya want it unloaded?"

"I'll have Duff help you," Case said, and turned away to search for Duff's whereabouts, missing the look that passed between Lily and the man.

The man's eyes followed the path of her scar, from the corner of her eye to the tip of her mouth. He frowned, ran a thumb unconsciously down his own cheek, took the toothpick from his mouth and turned his head, spitting onto the muddy ground as if to remove the bad taste of looking at Lily's disfigured face from his memory.

Lily smiled sarcastically and met his shocked expression with her head held high. She'd seen it all before.

"I'll see you later," Lily said, as she walked past Case, startling him with her short, clipped words and her angry stride.

He swerved around and caught the stare of the big, beefy delivery man's face. He was watching Lily's slender hips sway from side to side as she hurried toward the ranch house.

"Damn shame about her face," he said and stuffed the toothpick back in his mouth, sucking on the soggy corner with studied expertise. "She'd be real good looking 'cept for that gash on her cheek."

Case flushed a dark, angry crimson and doubled his fists before he even knew he'd moved. He knew Lily had heard every word the man said as her back stiffened and the distance between her steps increased.

"Shut your damn mouth," he muttered, eyes blazing, and walked right up to stare pointedly at the man's face, "unless you want to wear one just like it."

The man turned a pasty white, nearly choked on his toothpick and looked around for the person who was going to help him unload. He had a feeling he'd just put his size twelve foot into his mouth and if he didn't get the hell out of here fast, might just get Case Longren's boot in there, too.

"So, where's this Duff fellow anyway?" he muttered. "I got plenty more loads to haul. You ain't the only one who had storm damage last night."

Case motioned for Duff and then, after a quick set of instructions to his foreman, walked away from the delivery man before he did something to him that he might later regret. He wanted to go to Lily and reassure her that what the man had said about her did not matter to him in the least, but he knew now was not the time to do it. He could tell that simply by the way Lily had walked away. If she hadn't been a lady, he suspected she would have let the man have it with both barrels. It was all Case could do not to do it himself.

When he went to the house with the men later in the day to eat an early supper, Lily was all business. She wouldn't look at him and answered only in monosyllables. He sighed, choked down his food, unaware of what she'd even served, and knew he was back to square one. He could tell by the way she was acting that she'd just appointed herself judge and jury of their relationship and decided to put it to an early but painful death.

Case shoved his chair back from the table, carried his plate to the sink and slammed it down on top of several others.

Lily blinked and whirled around, thinking that someone had dropped and broken a plate. The look Case sent her way made shivers go all the way up her back in nervous anticipation. He obviously wasn't buying her silent treatment and, from the way he was staring, he was furious that she'd even tried it.

"I'm not about to put up with this 'sorry for myself attitude,' Lily Catherine," he muttered as he walked past her toward the door. "You're not getting out of last night this easy."

Lily swallowed back a shaky retort and watched him walk away in the growing dusk of nightfall. She didn't want out of anything. But she couldn't face the possibility of seeing a similar look of disgust on Case's face . . . ever. And the only way she could prevent that was to stay away from him altogether.

Lily spent a nervous evening and a lonely night, but Case didn't come into the den as usual to watch a weekly television show that they both enjoyed. He didn't show, by word or deed, that he even knew she was in the same house. Instead, when he finally came inside, footsteps dragging wearily, he walked up the staircase and out of her sight as if nothing had ever passed between them.

Lily stifled a sob, turned around and stared mutinously toward the television screen, refusing to admit, even to herself, that she deserved every bit of Case's disgust.

Finally, weary and heartsick, Lily made her way toward her own room beyond the kitchen, showered and then crawled into her bed with the soft, comforting mattress and freshly laundered sheets and wished for the ancient bedstead and the musty pillow-ticked mattress that she'd lain on the night before. And she longed for the man who'd lain beside her and loved her with a patience and a passion that she'd never believed existed.

"Goin' to town. Need anything?"

Case's question was short but less than sweet as he stared pointedly, waiting for Lily's answer.

Lily shoved aside the mountain of pie dough she'd just mixed and wiped her hands on the front of her apron.

"A couple of things," she answered quietly. "Do you mind going to the grocery store or would you rather wait and have me pick them up with the other foodstuffs later in the week?"

"Just give me the list," he said.

Lily handed him the paper with the list that she'd begun earlier. He caught it, along with her hand, and pulled her sharply toward him until they were nearly nose to nose.

Lily stared, transfixed, watching the shades of blue

in his eyes turning from dark and angry to white hot as he felt the whisper of her breath against his mouth.

"You're driving me crazy, lady. I look at you and all I can remember is how soft your body was beneath me, and how hot you got when I touched you."

It was the best . . . and the worst thing he could have said to her. It made her remember.

Lily swayed toward him as every muscle in her body went limp. Her eyelids drifted toward her cheeks in sleepy confusion as she watched Case's lips thin and his nostrils flare. It was the last thing she saw as he pulled her off the floor and into his arms.

His mouth moved across her lips, searching and taunting, until she opened her mouth beneath his touch, just as he demanded, and swallowed his urgent moan of need. She wrapped her arms around his neck and leaned into the strength of his body.

Everything Lily was, everything she'd ever wanted to be, revolved around the way this man was making her feel. His body swelled and hardened beneath her belly and Lily groaned in remembrance as he moved seductively against her, pressing himself into the part of her that burned for the man in her arms.

Then, as suddenly as he'd swooped, he stepped away, and Lily was left standing alone and aching as Case slid the list from her shaking fingers and smiled.

"I'll be back. Don't forget me while I'm gone."

Lily stared, stupefied by the absurdity of his remark. Forget Case Longren? Not in this lifetime. She buried her face in her hands and leaned back against the door facing as she heard him drive away. She was not going to survive this damnable roundup!

It was late as Case came down the hallway toward Lily's bedroom. His trip to town had been delayed by news he hadn't expected to face so soon. Lane Turney had met Case on the street, demanding back pay and his belongings that were still at the ranch.

The confrontation hadn't been pleasant, but it had served its purpose. Case had spent weeks telling himself what he would say to the man who'd frightened and shamed Lily so badly and then wrecked his car in the process.

Yet when the opportunity had arisen, all he'd been able to do was promise Turney if he ever so much as looked at Lily Brownfield again, there wouldn't be enough left of him for the coyotes to fight over.

Turney had turned several shades of red fury and stomped away, knowing that the man who'd been his boss meant every syllable of every word he'd just spit in his face.

"I still want my things," Turney had shouted over his shoulder as he'd hurried down the street, satisfied that he'd at least had the last word.

Case had completed his errands in brooding silence and hurried home, suddenly anxious to see Lily and reassure himself that she was all right. The memory of how close she'd come to harm at Lane Turney's hands still rankled and frightened him.

The main house was in darkness as he drove up; the only lights burning were in the downstairs hallway and in the wing where Lily was staying.

He put away the things she'd requested from town,

then picked up a small, flat box from the kitchen table and headed toward her room.

He walked up to her door, heard the sound of the shower running, and knew that she was already undressed and washing away the grit and grime of the day before retiring for bed. He groaned softly to himself, picturing the sight he knew he'd see if he'd only slip into the bathroom and into the shower with Lily. But it was too soon for familiarities such as that.

Yes, Lily had made love with him, but she'd also just as effectively shut him back out of her life. He had no intentions of rushing her into something she wasn't ready to face. Even if Case knew in his heart that she cared, he needed to hear the words from her own lips, not just feel it in the way she touched him.

He carefully turned the knob, peeked into her room, secure in the knowledge that he could complete his mission and leave before Lily exited her shower, and hurried over to the bed, anxious to leave his surprise.

Moments later, Lily turned off the water, grabbed for the bath towel and wrapped it around her body as she stepped out of the shower. She wrapped another, turban style, around her long, wet hair, and then began to dry herself before reaching for the hairdryer and the brush.

The steam was hot and thick in the tiny, enclosed bathroom, and Lily opened the door and left it ajar as she started the hairdryer. She leaned over, letting her hair fall loosely forward toward the floor as she moved the hot air above it in an unconscious rhythm.

It dried, and as it did, it fell in loose, taffy-colored waves, still clinging to her face and back in damp persistence. Lily straightened, and then stared as the steam slowly disappeared from the vanity mirror, revealing by its reflection the long, gossamer gown lying across the bed in the room behind her.

The dryer slipped from her hands and swiftly unplugged itself as it fell to the floor with a thud. The towel Lily had wrapped around her body loosened and slid to the floor beside it as she turned and stared.

It wasn't her imagination. It was strawberry silk, long and sheer, and Lily slid it up and over her head as if in a dream.

Case held his breath as he watched her walk across the floor toward her bed in unconscious abandon, oblivious of her own nudity as she picked up his gift and slid it over her bare body, lifting the heavy fall of her hair out from under the lace shoulder straps as she smiled softly in obvious delight.

Her hands slid down the length of the gown, from breasts to thighs, as she tested the satiny softness of its fabric against the palms of her hands. She closed her eyes, remembering the gown that Case had ripped from her body the night of the storm, and then turned at the thought of his name and knew he would be there.

Case took a deep breath as she turned toward him, met the wild green stare she sent his way as she realized he'd witnessed her state of undress, and shoved his fists as far down into his front pockets as they would go. God help him, he had to put them somewhere besides on Lily Brownfield.

Every sensuous movement of her body was accentuated by the fluidity of the pink silk that cupped and flowed around her like wind on water. Every muscle in his body expanded. If he had to walk, he would burst.

"It fits okay?" he asked, his voice quiet, anxious. She nodded.

"It's beautiful," Lily answered softly, and stroked her hands against her thighs, reveling in the feel of silk beneath her fingers.

"Just like you," Case answered, and then before Lily could answer or argue, he disappeared down the hallway.

Tears came so quickly, Lily didn't even know they were there until one fell from the corner of her mouth down onto the tip of one silk-covered breast, dotting the fragile fabric. A sob slipped up her throat and out into the quiet emptiness of her room. Lily shuddered, staggered backward until her legs felt the bed behind her and sank down in welcome abandon.

"Damn you, Case Longren," she muttered through tear-stained lips. "Damn you for making me believe you."

She rolled over on her side, drew herself up into a tiny pink ball of misery and cried herself to sleep.

Duff glared at Lane Turney as he swaggered and bragged while gathering his belongings. The sooner this man left the ranch, the better he'd feel. Something about him made Duff uneasy. He didn't know whether it was the fact that bad blood had already passed between him and the boss, or the fact that Turney's eyes kept sweeping toward the main house, obviously for a sight of Miss Lily. Either way, it would be none too soon for his liking when Turney left.

"You about through?" Duff asked sharply.

Turney glared, grabbed at his suitcase and jacket, and stomped toward the door, refusing to answer. He didn't owe this beat-up and aging excuse of a man the time of day.

He walked out into the sunshine, threw his belongings into the back of his pickup truck, and started around to the driver's side when one of the men came around the corner of the bunkhouse and shouted at Duff.

"Boss is looking for you," Pete called, pointing toward the corrals where some good-sized steers were being loaded into waiting trucks.

Duff stared pointedly at Turney, saw that he was getting into his truck, satisfied himself that his duty was done, and hurried to answer Case's call for help.

It was the opening that Turney had been waiting for. He slipped away from the truck, using the multitude of outbuildings for cover as he made his way toward the back of the lot where the herd bull was being kept. He'd make Longren sorry he'd refused to give him his back pay. He didn't buy the line that the vehicle he'd wrecked was worth ten times what had been owed him. He wanted revenge.

Turney couldn't mask the twinge of panic that twisted his gut as the huge dun-colored Brahman turned to watch his arrival.

The bull snorted and ducked his head, pawing at the ground with his forefeet as Turney moved toward the gate. Dust flew up and around his massive head, coating his long lop-ears and the huge hump on his back before drifting into his eyes and nostrils. It only served to make him madder.

Turney had a moment of regret after he slid the gate off the latch and then made a run for his truck.

The bull was so damn big and mean, but . . . Longren should have given him his money. He made a dive for the truck, started it and drove away in a cloud of red dust, leaving the Bar L and everyone on it as nothing more than bad memories.

The bull continued to bellow and paw at the ground, angered by the earlier presence of the man, as he butted and shoved at the heavy, metal rods of the corral fence. And then suddenly he was free! There was nothing between him and the sound of cows bawling but open space and dust. He tossed his head, snorting in angry abandon, and headed toward his herd with deadly, singleminded intent.

Case exited the walkway beside the loading chute and watched the last truck driving away to market with his steers. It was always a good feeling to know that he'd made it through another roundup. There wasn't much left to do after the steers were hauled off. In less than a week the roundup would be nothing but a tired memory, and the business of getting through a long, hot summer would be next on the agenda.

He took off his Stetson, slapping it against his leg as he walked to knock off the worst of the persistent dust, and headed toward the house. He was lost in thought, staring down at the ground as he walked, when he heard Duff yell. The sound of Duff's voice was high and strained, and the panic in it made Case's blood run cold.

When he looked up, he came face to face with the reason Duff and the men were screaming a warning.

The herd bull was loose! Less than fifty feet from Case stood a ton and a half of fury, head down, dust flying. A deep, angry bellow erupted from the belly of the animal and a shiver of dread ran all the way up Case's spine.

He looked frantically toward the house, knowing that the bull was between the yard and safety, looked back toward the corrals, their distance growing with every beat of his heart, and made his decision. He'd have to try and get back to the corrals. He had no choice.

It was the last thought Case had before the bull began to move, gathering momentum like a freight train out of control as he headed toward the man who stood between him and his herd.

Case flung his hat at the bull and pivoted toward the barns, running parallel to Duff and his men, and prayed. His long legs stretched with each panicked stride, but still the bull came on, and the distance shrank between them until Case could feel the ground beneath his feet vibrating from the bull's weight as he came on and on, faster and faster, with deadly precision.

It was an instant's knowledge that he wasn't going to make it, and with it the thought that he might never have that life with Lily after all.

Please God, if this is it, make it fast, Case prayed, and felt the whoosh of the bull's angry breath down the middle of his back.

NINE

Lily had just finished putting away the last of the pots and pans from the noon meal and was looking forward to her hour of free time before she had to worry about what to fix this evening.

She watched the last of the cattle trucks pulling away and knew that her time on the Bar L was quickly drawing to a close. Fingers of dread, regret, and something she refused to put a name to pulled her stomach into a knot. When the time came, she wasn't going to be ready to leave Case. But yesterday, the look of disgust on the deliveryman's face had gone a long way toward throwing Lily back into the state of mind in which she'd first arrived.

She slammed the cabinet door shut, wiped her damp hands on a kitchen towel and dropped it carelessly onto the countertop. Last night's sleeplessness wasn't helping matters either. Her eyes burned, and when she thought about it, tears kept puddling persistently.

Lily undid her apron, hung it across the back of a chair, then walked into the den. She pulled the tail of her mint green shirt out of its neat tuck inside matching striped slacks and started to kick off her shoes. It was the scream of a man in terror that stopped everything but her heart. What she saw as she pivoted toward the window nearly ended that function, too.

It was Duff that was screaming, yelling at the top of his voice, his little short legs churning up the dust as he ran. Other men were following closely behind, dragging ropes, waving their hands, yelling in unison as they tried to capture the attention of the dun-colored mass of fury that stood transfixed in the middle of the barnyard between the house and outbuildings.

It only took Lily a second to see what . . . or rather who . . . had captured the bull's attention. Case! His only avenue of safety cut off by the bull's presence.

"Nooo!" Lily groaned, as she watched the scene unfolding before her eyes.

The bull began to move just as Case flung his hat at it in a last-minute attempt to distract its attention and then everything seemed to happen in slow motion.

Her brain registered the fact that Case would never make it to the fences in time, just as she knew the men could not stop what was happening before their eyes.

And then a paperweight was lying on the floor in the midst of a shower of broken glass as her fingers closed around Case's hunting rifle, so like the one her brother, Cole, had taught her to use years ago.

The gun was loaded. Lily's quick check had assured her of that fact and she mentally thanked whoever had had the foresight to leave it locked away in that condition. If she'd had to search for, and then load ammunition, this race against time would have been futile.

Lily never remembered coming off the porch steps, nor flying through the gate surrounding the yard. She only had eyes for Case who was losing ground and the chance for life as the bull overtook his desperate vault to safety.

Case felt sweat coming out of his hairline and knew that it was going to burn like hell when it ran into his eyes. Yet he welcomed the thought knowing that it may well be the last conscious thing he ever experienced. Rage burned as his stride lengthened, yet he could tell without looking that he was losing ground. He wasn't ready to die. Not when he'd just been given a reason to live.

Lily!

An echo of thunder reverberated between the house and barnyard, mingling with the thud of Case's heartbeat, the pounding of the bull's hooves, and the rush of wind whistling in his ears as he made a frantic dive for the corral fence. He knew it was going to be short as the hot breath of the angry bull sent a deathly warning up the middle of his backbone.

Case gained the fence, shocked by the fact that he was still in one piece, and turned on the top rail, staring back in shock at the sudden silence of the scene frozen in still frame before his eyes.

His heart jumped to the bottom of his throat and tears burned the back of his nostrils as he shakily crawled down from the fence. He knew that Duff and Pete and the rest of his crew were talking and yelling in obvious relief, yet he could focus on nothing except the massive bull lying silent and still less than a foot from the place he'd jumped.

How?

He looked around in stunned confusion, and then nearly forgot to breathe as he saw Lily slump to her knees, drop his hunting rifle into the dust, and bury her face in her hands.

My God! My God! My Lily!

The prayer was as unconscious as his footsteps as he made his way around the mountainous form of the bull that lay harmlessly and lifelessly in the settling dust. He was heading for Lily.

"Boss! Boss!" Pete yelled, and he patted Case on the back as he and Duff came running up behind him. "Are you okay? Did you see that? She got him with one shot! Damn, you were a goner, sure as shootin'."

Case nodded, yet kept on walking, his focus entirely on the slender heap of the girl in green who was slumped in the dust.

"Get rid of that sonofabitch," Case muttered, and swung his arm back toward the dead animal. "Then tell the men to take the rest of the day off. I'll see them tomorrow."

"Whoopee," Pete yelled. "It's a story they won't believe in town. That's for damn sure. Our little California cook just saved the boss's life."

Their jubilant laughter and jesting faded away as Case came closer to Lily. He knelt beside her, pulled her hands away from her face and only then realized that she'd been crying in quiet desperation.

"Sweetheart," Case crooned, as he pulled her up

from the dust and into his arms. "My God, don't cry. Don't cry."

Lily shuddered as she heard his familiar voice and felt the comfort of his arms cradling her against his body. He was alive!

She'd been so afraid when she'd pulled the trigger. And when the gun had kicked against her shoulder and the bull had staggered in mid-stride and then dropped heavily into the dirt, a relief such as she'd never known had weakened every muscle in her body. She couldn't have stood upright after that to save her soul.

"I was afraid that I would hit you," she sobbed, as she buried her face into his chest, reveling in the smell of dirt, sweat, and the man who held her dearly.

She wrapped her arms around his waist and crushed him up against her with wild abandon. She didn't care who was watching, or what anyone thought. This man was her life. And he'd come so close to dying before her eyes she could still not believe he was safe.

"Come here, baby," he whispered softly against her ear. "You did fine. You did just fine."

He bent down, picked up his gun with one hand, wrapped his free arm around Lily's shaking shoulders, and guided her gently into the house.

It was cool and darker inside the house. And so still. Everything was focused, every heartbeat magnified, as Case shut the door behind them and then placed the gun inside a hall closet. He turned toward Lily who was still slumped against the wall of the hallway, staring at him with wide, wounded eyes as if she'd never get enough of looking. Her breath was ragged as the sobs slowly retreated back down her throat. She ran a shaky hand across her face, and then her fingers stilled as they unconsciously traced the thin red line across her cheek.

"Don't!" Case ordered harshly. "Not now, Lily Catherine! Not when everything nearly ended for us before it had a chance to begin."

She shuddered. Her hand stilled and then dropped limply to her side as she tilted her head against the wall behind her. She watched in fixation as Case came toward her. She'd seen that look on his face before. The night of the storm. And she was as helpless to deny him now as she had been then.

"Come with me," he coaxed, and when she hesitated, he swung her up into his arms and stalked toward the staircase as if she weighed nothing at all.

He carried her upstairs, down the hallway toward his room and into it, without a word passing between them. He kicked the door shut behind him, walked to his bed, and laid her down in the middle of a lake of black satin.

"I love you, Case Longren," Lily said softly, as her head touched his pillow.

There was no time left for pretense. Either he would accept her announcement or break her heart. It didn't matter. She could deny herself no longer.

"I know you do, Lily love," Case whispered, as his shirt fell to the floor. "And I love you, too. That you've always known. You just wouldn't accept it."

Lily smiled softly through a veil of tears and started to remove her clothing when Case stopped her with a look.

"Let me," he growled, and watched the pupils in Lily's eyes flare with undisguised passion.

Her hair fanned out over the satin like spilled mountain honey while Case removed each piece of her clothing as if it were made of glass. His gentleness was nearly her undoing as she watched the unsteady rise and fall of his chest beneath a wildly beating heart. Twice he had to pause and close his eyes, each time taking a deep, life-giving draught of air into his lungs to steady the shaking touch of his fingers.

Minutes ago he'd been near death. And then this woman beneath his hands had just handed his life, as well as her own love and life, right back to him. He could only bow to the strength of spirit it had taken for her to pull the trigger that saved him and the courage she'd shown by admitting her love. He was humbled at the thought of what he now possessed, yet he needed to be with Lily in a way that would confirm for them both, that life . . . and love . . . still existed.

And then she lay before him, ivory against midnight, highlighted in the white light of day . . . waiting . . . waiting.

The rest of his clothing fell to the floor. Case stood beside the bed and stared down at Lily, shaking, knowing that when he touched her he would not be able to slow down the immensity of emotion that was overwhelming him.

She sighed, held out her arms, and Case fell into them like a drowning man clutching at his only chance for survival. Their bodies met and melded, hands touching . . . seeking . . . feverishly assuring each other that life was still good.

Case wrapped his arms around her, rolled over and slid across the dark satin until he held Lily suspended above his waiting, aching body like an answer to his prayers.

His eyes grew dark, turning into the color of stormy evening, as he watched her breasts fall softly against the palms of his hands. He pushed them upwards, cupping the lush satiny globes as he rubbed a rough thumbprint across each swollen nub and rejoiced as he saw her body respond to his caresses.

Lily's breath caught in the back of her throat as Case teased at the tips of her breasts. She moved hungrily against the thrust of his body beneath her hips.

She moaned, her body arching, as Case shifted, pulling her up and then settling her down upon him in a slow, sensuous movement that drove sanity out and pulled madness in.

Case held his breath, gritted his teeth, and willed himself not to explode as Lily settled around him. Her body moved beneath his hands, responding to his every urgency, reveling in the command of his touch.

"You're not leaving me," Case whispered through tightly clenched lips as he held her pinioned by the thrust of his body.

Lily opened her eyes, looked down, and fell into a world of blue where only she and her man existed.

She sighed, nodding slowly as he moved his hands down past her belly, wrapped his hands tightly at the bend of each thigh and let his thumbs taunt at the hidden mysteries of Lily Brownfield.

"Never," she promised. "Now love me, cowboy, before I go mad."

There, while the sunlight spilled across black satin, Case Longren branded his L.A. woman with a love and devotion that left her sobbing and sighing and begging for more.

There could be no more doubt in Lily's mind that Case would only love her in the dark. He took her to heaven and back with the sun on her hair and his hands on her face. And when he was through, he lay down beside her and watched her cry herself to sleep. It was only after she'd succumbed to the exhaustion of terror and the delight of his love, that Case could let himself go, too.

He wrapped his fists into the tangle of her hair, turned her in his arms, chest to breast, and cried.

Quietly . . . steadily.

It was revealing . . . and healing . . . and soon Case, too, was asleep as the evening sun slid slowly toward the horizon.

"I will call your father tomorrow," Case said quietly, as he watched Lily slowly come awake in his arms. "I'm not going to ask him, I'm going to tell him. You're going to marry me . . . tomorrow . . . next week . . . next month. I don't care where, but it damn well better be soon. I'm not sleeping alone another night, Lily love. I'll never let you out of my arms again."

"Hello to you, too," she said softly with a smile, and pulled his mutinous mouth slowly toward her. "And yes, thank you, I believe I will."

The look on his face was worth a thousand words as Lily let her head fall back onto the bed, and she laughed until he silenced her with his mouth, and then his hands, and then his body.

Life was good.

The next morning at breakfast Duff took one look

at Lily, another at the boss, and smiled. His face broke into a thousand tiny wrinkles of joy, and his eyes nearly disappeared beneath the tangle as he slapped his leg with glee.

"What's so funny?" Pete grumbled, frowning as one of the men in line behind him jammed a fork in a plate of bacon and came away with more than his share of breakfast.

"We got ourselves a cook!" he crowed.

"Hell's fire, man, have you gone and lost your mind?" Pete grumbled. "We've had a cook . . . all during roundup."

"I mean . . . we got us a cook . . . for life," Duff mumbled beneath his breath, and nudged Pete to look toward their boss who was brushing a trace of flour gently off of Lily's chin.

Pete's mouth dropped open, and he forgot to be mad that two more men just pushed past him in line.

"Hot damn," he whispered back. "No more boiled beef and stewed prunes for us, Arloe. We're eatin' high on the hog now."

The two old friends grinned and nudged as they collected their breakfast and went off to work later with a lilt in their voices and a kick to their steps.

The boss was due some good luck. And Lily Brownfield was *some* good luck. Not only was she pretty, she could cook and she could shoot. What more could a man want, they asked themselves?

Lily didn't know it, but she'd just fallen in love with a man and a state that had no need for a feminist movement. Here women had always been equal, whether they'd wanted it or not. They'd had to be. From pioneer days onward. They'd tilled the land, and borne the children. They'd roped the cattle and built fences. They could ride, and they could fight, and they knew when it was time to love. Whether they were oil producers or ranchers, business women or homemakers, they made their choices and their men stood by them. They were a stubborn, proud, and hardy race of women, and Lily Brownfield fit in like the last piece of a puzzle.

"Pete knows," Lily said, as she watched the men walk away with their heads together.

"So does Duff," Case grinned. "It's no wonder. I can't get this bedroom look off my face, Lily love. You've branded me for life."

Lily blushed and swiped at him with the dish towel.

"Get out of my kitchen, mister," she teased. "I've got work to do."

"We call your dad, this evening," Case reminded her.

Lily nodded, and tried to hold back the tears. She couldn't believe she was this happy. She was afraid to count her blessings.

"Wipe that look off your face, girl," Case growled and pulled her into his arms. "I don't have time to remind you how you drive me crazy. We've got to finish up the last of the storm repairs before the extra help is gone."

"I wasn't doubting you, Case," she said softly as she slid her hands around his back and down into his hip pockets, pulling their lower bodies into sensuous alignment. "It's just leftover memories."

"If I ever get the chance, I will personally rearrange Todd Collins's body. He'll have a hell of a time getting clothes to fit him when he finds my boot permanently up his . . ."

"Case!"

The look of amused shock on Lily's face was worth it. Case grinned wickedly, cupped her face and leaned forward. He could hardly wait for the rest of his life. One minute a teasing temptress, the next a prim and proper lady. He'd never know what to expect.

"And that's a promise," he repeated, branded her with a sultry kiss, and followed his men to the day's work.

Morgan Brownfield hung up the phone with a smile on his face and a light in his eyes. He turned around, faced his brood of sons and grinned widely.

"Cole wins," he announced. "He said Case would call before the month was over. Personally I gave him until July. I guess I underestimated either Lily . . . or him. Either way, we're getting ourselves another member of the family." And then he turned and fixed Cole with a telling expression. "And, Cole, it seems that your target practice with Lily finally paid off. He said she saved his life . . . with one shot."

Cole Brownfield grinned as he buckled on his shoulder holster and then punched his pistol into the case laying just below his armpit. Pride welled within him. Lily was a special sister . . . in more ways than one.

"Told you Lily was in love," he said softly. "Hey, Buddy!" he yelled, as he stuffed his badge into his jacket pocket and waited for his absent-minded but brilliant brother to emerge from his makeshift office off the kitchen.

Buddy Brownfield stuck his head out of the door and shoved his glasses on top of his head.

"What's the big deal?" he yelled. "I was right in the middle of something."

"You're always in the middle of something," the twins taunted. "Lily Kate is getting married," they said in unison.

"I knew that," Buddy sighed, and pulled his glasses back on his nose. "When an immovable object meets an unstoppable force . . ."

"For pete's sake, Buddy," Morgan muttered in disgust at his second son. "They're in love."

Buddy rolled his eyes before slipping back into his room.

"That's just what I was saying," he muttered beneath his breath. "It would be nice if just once, *just once*! . . . someone understood plain English around here."

The Brownfield men stared first at the door as it closed in their faces and then back at each other. They burst out laughing. Buddy was Buddy, and their world was back on track. Case Longren would take care of their Lily for the rest of her life. Of that they had no doubt. Of that they were glad.

"Where do you want to hold the wedding?" Case asked, as he watched Lily deftly twisting her long, silky hair into a neat braid, and he resisted the urge to stop her hands and take it all back down again. "I don't mind traveling to L.A. with you if that's what you want. After all, that's where most of your friends must be."

Lily's hair mesmerized him. It was his favorite thing about her. He didn't care how she wore it, he just wanted it to be the only thing she was wearing. Making love to Lily was becoming an addiction. But she hadn't complained yet, so he had no intentions of bringing anything to a halt.

Lily smiled softly and turned to face Case who was stretched out full-length on his back, on her bed, watching her finish her morning routine.

"You're wrong, mister," Lily said. "Most of my friends seem to be here in Oklahoma. They may be new, but they've been truer friends than any I've left behind. My dad and brothers will fly out. I don't have any other close relatives. How about you?"

Case grew solemn. This was something he and Lily had never discussed, but if she was going to be the other half of his heart, it was time she knew what she'd tied herself to.

"As you know, my dad died several years ago."

Lily nodded, sensing that the light manner in which the conversation had begun had just taken a more serious note.

Case took a deep breath, arose from Lily's bed, and walked over to stare sightlessly out her bedroom window. He didn't see the bright sun climbing relentlessly upward, nor the hummingbirds darting in and out of the feeders that Duff kept strung across the back porch.

He was seeing another time long ago when clouds rolled across the sky and a bolt of lightning bounced across the prairie as his mother flung herself from the porch. She was running toward their old Chevy, out into the oncoming storm, her screams of anger lost in the rush of the wind and the pounding of his heart.

Chock Longren stood silent in the onslaught that

was tearing his world apart. He'd seen it coming but he'd been unable to stop her growing dissatisfaction with a lifestyle that had been sparse and hard.

Carrie Longren had driven away without ever looking back. Case had long ago forgotten what his father had said by way of excuse. But he'd never forgiven his mother for what it had done to the once proud man. Case had watched his dad turn hard, bitter, and drunk by degrees, until there wasn't a shadow of his former self alive. Case didn't know where his mother was, and as God was his witness, he didn't care. He just didn't know if he could make Lily understand. Her family was so close.

Case turned away from the window and fixed Lily with a hard, piercing stare.

"I don't know if you're going to understand this, but believe me, I mean every word I'm saying." He took a deep breath. "My dad is dead . . . but my mother's not. At least I don't think she is. And frankly, I couldn't care less."

"Case!"

Lily's shocked response was expected.

"I was nineteen years old when she walked out on Dad and me without ever looking back. It killed him, and . . . well . . . I grew up pretty fast. She wasn't much of a mother to begin with. She didn't ever go for this life. But she damn well could have kept in touch with me. She didn't, and I quit caring years ago."

Lily was in his arms. The hurt was still there. He just didn't know it. She heard it swell within him as the words boiled out of his mouth and she knew that it would take her a lifetime of loving to wipe away the pain of abandonment he'd suffered.

A sweet, deep feeling of belonging swept over her as she slid her mouth across the base of his throat. His pulse was throbbing beneath her lips as she leaned back and pulled his face toward her.

"I'm so sorry, my darling," Lily whispered. "But you've got me. And I swear by all that's holy that you'll never see me leave. Not until God himself comes and takes me. For as long as we have, you have me."

Case groaned. Her words were too much, just as the depth of her loving.

"I know that, Lily Catherine. And I thank you . . ." his voice broke, as he wrapped her in a hug before he continued. "And you'll never be sorry you trusted me."

Lily grinned, instantly sensing that it was time to lighten the mood.

"Oh," she teased, as she moved gently back and forth against the bulge below his belt buckle, "I'm glad about a whole lot of things, cowboy. One being . . ."

She never got to finish her statement. Case had her in his arms and back in bed.

"Are you undressing me again?" Lily asked in mock disgust. She could hardly wait.

"Yep," Case said solemnly, as he deftly removed the clothes she'd just put on. "And I'm real sorry, Lily Kate, but your hair's comin' down, too."

"Lord have mercy," Lily moaned in fake distress. "What's a lady to do?"

"Honey," Case breathed across her breasts and watched in delight as they peaked to attention. "Being a lady has nothing to do with this. Nothing at all."

Lily gasped in delight as Case's hands slid across her body.

He was absolutely right!

It was hours later when Case shoved a pillow beneath his head, propped himself up on one elbow and ran his forefinger from the tip of her chin, down her neck, between the valley of her breasts, circled the dip of her belly button, and started toward territory that Lily knew would only prolong their day in bed.

She grabbed his hand just before it got them both into trouble, and muttered, fixing him with a sharp, green stare.

"Case! We've just made love enough for three honeymoons, and we still don't have the wedding planned."

"Oh, honey," Case whispered as his mouth lowered toward that teasing tip of breast closest to his lips. "If you think this is too much, just wait. You plan the wedding. I'm looking on to better things. Like the wedding night."

Lily sighed. "You won't be disappointed? We've kind of . . . well, we've already . . ."

Case laughed. They were buck naked, they'd made love twice this morning and many times before, and all of a sudden she was shy. He loved his L.A. lady. She was a constant mixture of contradictions.

"Yeah, we did," he grinned. "But there's ways you've never even heard of . . . let alone participated in, Lily, love. I'm saving them for the wedding night."

"Well, I never!" she gasped and stared, uncertain whether to be shocked or excited.

"I didn't think so," Case grinned again. "But you will, Lily. You will."

The promise was one to sleep on.

Halfway across the continent Todd Collins slammed down the phone and leaned back in his powder blue executive's chair and ran his fingers across the expensive leather. He stared at the perfectly coordinated furnishings and frowned. Nothing was going according to plan.

He'd expected to get the junior partner's position a month ago, and instead Marve Leedy had been chosen. They'd patted Todd on the back, murmured comforting things about working hard and hoping that everything panned out soon, but it had only been platitudes and he knew it.

He knew exactly when his plans for advancement had gone awry and it had begun the moment he'd let Lily give him back his ring. His bosses had been dismayed to learn of their breakup, and Todd had felt an instant rebuff when he'd mentioned her face and how he'd wanted her to get it fixed before they'd married. If she hadn't been so hasty, and if he'd just had time to think it over. He knew once he'd had time to digest the fact that Lily was permanently scarred that he could have learned to live with it. They were doing wonders with makeup these days. After all, he was living in the movie capital of the world. There wasn't anything they couldn't do with a little bit of plastic and some greasepaint. Surely something could have been done to disguise Lily's disfigurement.

A deep feeling of panic began to form in the pit of his stomach. Some instinct told him that if he ever expected to make it in this firm, he had some fence mending to do with Lily Brownfield.

She had been a very well-liked employee, and the fact that their engagement had ended promptly on the note that she'd been scarred had not set well with the powers that be. More than once he'd caught people staring at him. And he knew he wasn't imagining it when a conversation would suddenly cease upon his entering a room.

Well, he just wasn't having it. Not any of it. He'd simply have to find Lily and get her back. It would be easy. Once she knew how he felt, he was certain that she'd be more than happy to take him back. After all, he thought, as he shuffled through his Rolodex for her father's home number, who else would want her?

TEN

Todd kept one eye on the traffic and the other on the freeway signs overhead. He didn't want to miss the one that would take him into Laguna Beach.

He'd made a phone call to Lily's beachfront home, thinking that he would begin the mending of their relationship there, but his plans had gone awry when a strange woman had answered the phone.

The ditzy female had informed him in the worst "valley girl" accent he'd ever heard, that "Lily was . . . like, not here . . . and that . . . she was, like . . . gone for the summer."

Todd could only assume that Lily had gone home to Laguna Beach to be with her family. He could hardly blame her. If spending the summer with Mitzi was her only option, he'd have gone, too. He'd hung up in disgust. It was his opinion that people like Mitzi gave Californians a bad name.

Todd frowned and ran his fingers through his blond hair in practiced perfection as he drove. He'd only been to Lily's home twice and both times she'd been driving, so he watched the road carefully for the proper signs that would alert him which highway to take.

After the last time, he'd had no desire to go back again. Her brothers didn't like him. Not one bit. And he wasn't so sure about her father, either. He'd spent their entire last visit wondering if Cole was going to slap him in handcuffs and drop him in the ocean, or if Buddy was going to stage an accidental electrocution with some of his damnable computer equipment. It was all over the place. Just like the Brownfield men. Everywhere he'd turned, there'd been at least one of them. And when her twin brothers had arrived, Todd had been at his wits' end. Two of them, looking alike, thinking alike, and with equally conniving minds, had been the last straw. He'd insisted that they leave. Right then and there. By that time, even Lily had seen the wisdom of the decision. The only thing that aggravated Todd was the fact that Lily thought their behavior amusing.

Suddenly the exit came into view, and Todd took the turn with his heart in his mouth. He didn't know who'd be there when he arrived, but he hoped it would only be Lily. He didn't want to face any of her family just yet. Not until he and Lily had made up. And it would happen. Of that, he was totally convinced.

The last person Cole Brownfield expected to see at the front door was Lily's ex-fiancé, Todd Collins. He didn't know whether to just hit him now, or wait until he'd opened his mouth. If he hit him now, he'd only bust his lip. If he waited until he opened his mouth to talk, maybe it would loosen a few of those perfectly capped teeth in the process.

Todd saw the look of anger sliding across Cole's face and held up his hands in mock surrender.

"Now, Cole," he said, flashing his famous smile. "I've come to see Lily. Surely you wouldn't begrudge me the chance to make up for any misunderstandings that have come between us."

"You what?" Cole muttered. He couldn't believe his ears.

"I want to see Lily," Todd repeated. "I've missed her terribly. I can't wait to see how she's doing. I don't suppose she's mentioned me?"

"I don't suppose," Cole drawled.

Todd suppressed a groan of dismay.

"So . . . would you tell Lily I'm here?" Todd continued.

"Can't."

Todd rolled his eyes. This brother was the most damnable of the lot. He was the oldest, the most arrogant, and . . . the most likely to shoot! He'd just remembered that Cole Brownfield was a policeman. It wouldn't do to antagonize him.

"Why can't you, Cole? Is Lily asleep . . . shopping . . . ?"

"She's gone. She's out of state."

If Cole had announced that Lily had gone to the moon, Todd would have been no less surprised.

"Gone?" Todd mumbled.

Cole nodded. A sudden inspired thought just took hold. Maybe he wouldn't hurt Todd Collins after all. Maybe he'd just tell him where Lily really was. He remembered the predatory manner in which Case Longren had greeted them on their arrival to the ranch. He could hear the menace in Case's voice now as he'd threatened them all when he thought one of them had been Lily's ex-fiancé.

"Actually, she's in Clinton, Oklahoma. Well, no . . . that's not *exactly* accurate," Cole mumbled, and leaned against the doorjamb, delighting in the nervous way Todd Collins kept watching him, making sure that there was just enough distance between them to maintain a level of safety.

"Where *exactly* is she?" Todd persisted. "I need to see her. It's a matter of extreme importance."

"Important, you say?" Cole muttered. "Well, since you put it that way, I guess I have no choice."

Todd sighed. Now he was getting somewhere.

"What's the address?" Todd asked, pulled out a notebook and pen, and poised it above a clean sheet of paper.

"It's not exactly an . . . address," Cole continued. "She's on a ranch outside of the town . . . working as a cook . . . for spring cattle roundup."

Todd poked a hole in the clean sheet of paper with his pen. His mouth dropped and his eyes rolled back in his head, and if Cole hadn't known better, he would have thought that old Todd "The Bod" Collins had just had a stroke.

"Cook? Ranch? Roundup? Oh my God! What have I done? How can I reach her? I had no idea!"

This was getting better and better. Cole could hardly contain his glee. And he wished with everything he owned that he could be a fly on the wall when Case Longren and Todd Collins met face to face for the first time.

"Sure thing, Todd. Just give me the paper. I'll write down the directions. We were out there about a month ago. Quite a place. They had a barbecue for us when we were there, but the food is a bit strange.'' Cole lingered over his warning for effect. ''One of the main choices on the menu was calf fries. Ever had them? All they do is . . .''

By the time Lily's brother had handed the paper back, Todd had turned twelve shades of green. Cole Brownfield knew he'd done his duty. He hadn't been able to punch Todd Collins in the face, but he'd just set him up for something better.

Todd ran back to his car and slid in behind the wheel. He had it made. Lily had to be desperate. All he had to do was show up. She'd be begging him to take her back. And when he did, it would only be a matter of time before he had that partnership in his pocket.

Yes, things were finally going his way.

''You're getting married?''

Debbie Randall squealed with glee as Lily grinned and pushed the much smaller basket of foodstuff through Debbie's checkout lane. The extra crew was gone, only one or two of the other men lingered as Duff had them finishing particular jobs. Spring roundup was over, and Lily's life was just beginning.

''We called Dad and the boys, but nothing's been set. However, I doubt if we wait long. Case isn't into waiting . . . at least not about . . .''

Lily blushed and Debbie grinned. ''I'll just bet,'' she crowed as she quickly shoved Lily's purchases through the scanner. ''Oooh, goody!'' Debbie cried. ''If your family comes back, then that means *all* your family.''

Lily rolled her eyes and resisted the urge to laugh. She'd been hearing that line all her life. If it wasn't one, it was any of the three other Brownfields. Frankly Lily couldn't see what was so interesting. Cole was bull-headed, Buddy was lost in a world of his own, and J.D. and Dusty didn't have time for anyone but themselves.

"Yes, that means the twins are coming back, too," Lily laughed, assuming that they were the object of Debbie's delight.

Debbie cocked an eyebrow, hit total on the cash register, and said, "That'll be $82.53, and what makes you think I'm talking about the twins?"

Now it was Lily's turn to be dumbfounded. "But I thought . . . I mean they left you that note . . . I just assumed . . ."

Debbie shook her head and smiled secretively.

"Never you mind," she said. "I'm just glad they're coming back."

Lily signed the charge slip, watched Debbie pull the next basket of groceries into her lane, and wave a happy good-bye.

Case pulled up into the loading lane and jumped out, opened the trunk of the car, and kissed Lily soundly as the bag boy stuffed the sacks into the trunk.

"Case," Lily mumbled, straightening her clothing as Case reluctantly released her and ushered her toward the passenger side of the car. "Someone will see."

He grinned and waved to Debbie who was pointing and laughing at them from behind the wide expanse of storefront plate glass.

"Someone already did."

Lily laughed helplessly, turned and waved, and hastened into the car. The sooner she got Case out of the public eye, the safer.

"Debbie likes one of my brothers," Lily remarked, as they drove through the busy traffic and headed for the ranch.

Case cocked an eyebrow, leaned his head back against the headrest of the car as he drove, and thought for a moment. Then he smiled, turned and sent Lily a look that made her lean over and turn the air conditioner on high.

"It's Cole."

His announcement couldn't have surprised her more if he'd claimed it to be her father.

"No way," Lily argued.

"Yep, it's Cole." He wouldn't be budged.

"So, what makes you think that, O learned one?"

"They ignored each other. Ignoring someone's existence is a sure sign of attraction."

"Pooh!" Lily huffed. "You didn't ignore me."

Case sighed as they turned into the driveway of the Bar L and headed for home.

"That's true, but it wasn't my fault."

Lily's mouth dropped. She turned at least three shades of red and then she huffed.

"You're saying it was mine? That I chased you? That I wouldn't let you ignore me?"

She folded her arms across her chest and glared out the window as they came to a stop. Case leaned over, opened the glove box and pushed a button inside. The trunk of the car automatically popped up. Case looked wickedly up at Lily's fuming expression.

"Hell, honey! What was I to do? You waited until

there was a tornado overhead, hail raining down like bullets, and me helpless and wet. And that bed . . . well . . . it just wasn't my fault. I didn't have anywhere to run.''

The expression on her face was priceless. Case laughed all the way to the house, but when they got inside, he was left alone to put up their foodstuffs while Lily stomped off to her room. Case grinned. He knew Lily. She wasn't really mad. She just didn't have a real argument to refute his teasing.

He slammed the refrigerator door shut, put the last can of peaches into the cabinet, and neatly folded the paper sacks that had come from the market. He heard a sound behind him, and turned.

The breath whooshed out of his lungs in the flash of a heartbeat. He dropped the paper sack on the floor, as he was mesmerized by the sight of Lily standing before him wearing the sheer pink nightgown he'd purchased for her days earlier.

Her hair hung down upon her shoulders like sunny silk, her feet were bare, and if his eyes weren't deceiving him, so was everything else beneath that passion in pink.

"Here I am, cowboy," Lily said softly. "And there's three doors in this house and all the sunlight you could want. Either run or do your duty."

"Oh my God!" Case groaned, as his body reacted to the sight of all that pink . . . and Lily.

"I'm waiting," she teased gently.

"Not for long," he muttered, as he swept her into his arms and headed for her bedroom.

"Case . . . darling . . . I had something else in mind," Lily whispered in his ear. "I just love making love . . . on that black satin on your bed."

Case groaned again. Black satin indeed! He would be lucky to make it down the hall to her bedroom, let alone climb a flight of stairs first.

"Later, love," he muttered, as he laid her down upon her bed. "Later. Right now, I've waited far too long as it is."

Lily smiled. She watched Case shedding his clothes like water and knew by the condition he was in when he came down to her that he was speaking the truth.

There were no lingering touches, no whispered words of endearment. Only Case sliding the pink silk up as he slid into Lily. She moaned once, and then all was silent as Case covered her mouth with his own. It was swift, and sudden . . . a flash of heat burst through her as Case thrust wildly, arched his back, and shuddered as he gave up to the madness.

And then there was silence in the room as Case came slowly back to earth, sanity returning with a calmer heartbeat, and the gentle, assuring stroke of Lily's hands upon his back.

"What just happened?" Case groaned against her breasts, as he buried his face in their ivory cushion.

"Case, darling," Lily said softly against his ear.

"What?" he muttered as his bones quietly turned to mush.

"You're real good at duties."

He grinned.

"Thank you, Lily Catherine."

She smiled to herself as he nuzzled against her and closed his eyes with a sigh.

"You're very welcome," she said.

*   *   *

Lily watched Case walking toward his pickup truck and knew that he was going to be away from the ranch for at least a couple of hours. She wrung her hands nervously and knew that if he suspected what she had in mind, he'd kill her. After all the preaching he'd done about loving her the way she was, he would think she didn't believe a word he'd said. But that wasn't it. Lily knew now, if she knew nothing else in life, that Case Longren loved her.

But Lily wanted to know. She needed to know. She watched him driving away and made a run for the den. She wanted some privacy when she made her call.

She'd snuck the first of her trips to a local plastic surgeon during a trip to the market. The second of her visits had coincided with a trip to the beauty shop. She had only a phone call to make before she decided if there would be a third trip.

She dialed, identified herself, asked to speak to Dr. Calloway, and then waited. When he came on the line, Lily held her breath, and then a smile began. First in her eyes, then on her face, and finally in her heart, until she feared she would burst from the joy.

She was ready! Her face was healed enough that he strongly recommended some corrective surgery. And although he was professionally cautious, he predicted wonderful results.

She hung up the phone with a promise to get back with him. First things first. Now she knew it could be done. She just had to convince Case how important it was for her to feel the best she could be, not because she feared he wouldn't love her, but because he did in spite of it.

Todd Collins turned back onto the main highway and sighed in disgust. That was the fourth wrong turn he'd made trying to find this damnable Bar L ranch where Lily was supposed to be.

If it was anything like the last two at which he'd stopped, she'd run over him trying to get to the car. He'd never seen so much dust and livestock in his life.

The last stop he'd made, the dog had nearly torn his arm to shreds. And he thought he'd heard glass breaking when the dog had jumped at the headlight of his car. All he'd done was stick his arm from the window to try and get the owner's attention. People shouldn't be allowed to have such vicious animals. It was his fervent belief that things that barked and growled should be no more than twelve inches tall and could be held in one's lap. Not large enough to eat one's headlights. But, he muttered to himself as he started back down the highway, at least he now knew where the Bar L was located. He watched the road for the landmark the rancher had indicated and turned into the long, narrow, graveled road with something akin to relief. He was almost there. It would be none too soon when he got Lily back to L.A. with him where she belonged, and pulled his life back into the order he so desired.

Lily heard the car coming down the drive. It didn't sound like Case's Ford. She smiled to herself as she started toward the window. She was becoming a real rancher's woman, recognizing vehicles by sound and not sight.

The sedan was covered in dust, a headlight was broken, and the sun glared down onto the windshield so that Lily couldn't tell if it was a man or a woman inside.

She walked out onto the porch, stepped down on the first step and shaded her eyes with her hand as she propped her other on the curve of her hip.

Todd was shocked at the pull of lust he felt as he saw Lily standing tall, and tanned, waiting for him. A vision in pink and white. She looked so . . . he couldn't believe it . . . but she looked wonderful!

Oh my sweet Lord! Lily muttered to herself. *It's Todd!*

And then a slow, burning anger began, and it spread throughout Lily's body until she felt as if she'd just been flashfired and tossed aside. How dare he!

"Lily! Darling!"

Todd made what he assumed was a romantic dash toward Lily who stood obviously awaiting his ascent to the steps.

"What the hell are you doing here?" she snarled.

Todd couldn't have been more surprised. Lily didn't talk like that. The Lily he'd known didn't curse, or glare . . . or . . . God help him, double up her fists. What had happened to the sweet, pliable young thing he'd known?

"Now, Lily," he began. "I know you have reason to be angry, but I've reconsidered our relationship and . . ."

"We don't have a relationship," Lily said quietly. "You decided that . . . remember?"

Todd's gut kicked into low gear. This wasn't going exactly as he'd imagined.

"I know, and I'm just devastated," Todd said with what he hoped was heartfelt abjectness. "All I can say is . . . I must have been in shock. I don't know what I was thinking. But I know why I'm here. I'm going to take you away from all this . . . all this . . ."

He waved his arms, unable to put words to the thought of her working as a drudge for a bunch of ruffians.

Case's pickup topped the hill above home, and he frowned at the sight of a strange car parked in the yard. The closer he got, the more certain he became that Lily was involved in some sort of confrontation. He pressed on the gas. He knew that Lane Turney was gone for good. He couldn't imagine who . . .

Sunlight bounced off of perfectly groomed, sun-bleached blonde hair, tanned skin, and a mouthful of teeth that had to have been capped. Case could see them from here. He climbed out of the truck, shoved his hat down firmly upon his dark hair, and stalked toward Lily. Blue fire burned.

Todd turned. He forgot to breathe, and then when he did, his question came out three octaves higher and in one long rush.

"Who's that?" he squealed.

"That's what you want to take me away from," Lily drawled, and knew that justice did come to those who wait.

Every plan, every dream, every hope Todd Collins had for a better tomorrow just hit the dust with his guts. He didn't know whether to stand or run. Either way, his hope of taking Lily Brownfield away from "all this" just disappeared.

At least six and a half feet of pure fury was stalking toward him with malice aforethought. He could see it in the blue shards piercing his soul.

"If he hits me, I'm suing," Todd shrieked, and pointed wildly toward Case, who was coming nearer and nearer.

It was the last straw. Lily lost sight of reason. She wouldn't have Case threatened in any way. She growled low in her throat, doubled up her fist, and came flying off the porch steps.

"Then sue me, you jerk."

Todd didn't see it coming, but Case did. He knew by the look on her face that Lily had lost it. And, he knew that he'd never get to her in time to stop it from happening.

Todd's nose scrunched beneath her knuckles, and he staggered, falling backward into the honeysuckle. He started to yelp when blood began oozing out from his left nostril, but then he gasped instead. "You bloodied my nose!" Todd couldn't believe it had happened.

"And I'm going to do it again," Lily shrieked. She fell down upon him, fists flailing the vines and the blooms, as Todd's moans of pain and his shrieks of panic were lost in her anger.

Case grinned. This was the best medicine Lily could have ever received. This would heal the scars inside her heart as nothing else could. He stood back, hands on hips, arms akimbo, and watched with pride as Lily got in several more good blows. Finally, he decided it was time to save Todd Collins. After all, there had to be enough of him left to ship back to L.A. He didn't want to have to bury the sonofabitch here on the Bar L. Knowingly contaminating land was against the law.

"Lily! Darlin'! Let him up," Case muttered, as he bent down and grabbed her shoulders, dodging a wild fist as he pulled her up and out of the honeysuckle. When Lily could no longer attack Todd with her fists, she went after him with words.

Todd had never heard so many curse words, at one time, from one woman, in his life. And the look of fury in the cold blue eyes of the man who'd just saved him from a fate worse than death didn't assure him one iota that he was safe yet.

Case cast one wary eye toward Lily and the other at the sodden lump crawling out of his honeysuckle bush. The perfectly combed hair was no more. Instead it hung limply in his eyes. Leaves were stuck in the collar of his blue Polo shirt and in his hair, and grass stains graced both knees of his white Calvin Klein slacks. Dirt smudges were all over his elbows and face, mixing marvelously with the steady streams of blood that dripped from his lips and nose.

"Are you all right, darlin'?" he asked quietly, and turned another anxious look Lily's way.

"Is she all right? Is *she* all right? Have you lost your mind? Look at me! I'm the one who needs attention!"

Todd crawled to his feet and then knew retreat would have been the better part of valor.

"You want attention?" Case asked quietly . . . too quietly.

Todd shook his head, but it was too late. Attention had already come.

"You think you're the one who's been harmed here?"

Todd shook his head again, and began backing toward his rental car. He knew he was never going to make it. It was too far to L.A. and the big man was too close for comfort.

"I'll show you harm, you slimy weasel," Case muttered, as he picked Todd up by the collar and dragged him backwards toward his car, slammed him up against the door and bent down and whispered in his ear.

Lily saw Todd take one panicked look up at Case's face, and then he all but crawled through the open window of his car. He scrambled inside.

A laugh began so deep inside her that Lily knew that every pain she'd ever had since her accident was going to come out with it. She remembered what Case had promised to do if he should ever meet her ex-fiancé. She absently wondered if Case's boot would actually fit, as Todd's little rear disappeared into the car. He drove off in a fit of panic.

Case turned around. The sound behind him was like nothing he'd ever heard.

Lily was laughing.

Not smiles, not the gentle giggle he'd heard from time to time. It was a roll on the grass, head back, belly laugh that sent her to her knees. Tears streamed out of her eyes, running little clean tracks through the dirty smudges on her face as she wrapped her arms around her middle and doubled over with uncontrolled mirth. Several times she'd point down the road, mumble something through her hysterics, and then sink back on her heels, helpless to do anything else but give way to the release that her body needed.

"Oh, Lordy," she sighed, as she struggled to crawl to her feet. "Help me, you moose. I'm too weak to stand."

"Help you?" Case smiled, as he pulled her into his arms. "You didn't look like you needed much help. You did real fine, Lily Kate. Real fine."

"I did, didn't I," Lily said wistfully and stared back over her shoulder at the swiftly settling dust of Todd's departure. "It wasn't the most ladylike thing I've ever done." And then she smiled. "But Cole would have been proud."

"Not as proud as I was, Lily. Not nearly as proud. Sometimes being a lady isn't nearly as important as being a woman. Do you know what I mean?"

Case's question was serious, but his eyes were still alight with glee.

Lily took a deep breath, wrapped her arms around him, and released her breath in a sigh.

"I know what you mean, Case. And, I think that I just passed my test with flying colors." She grinned. "Yesterday I was but a lady. Today I became a woman."

Case laughed. Pulled her up, off her feet and into his arms.

"You're a woman all right, Lily Catherine. My woman! Come on. I've got to get you inside and cleaned up. We've got places to go and people to see. After today, I think you've just earned yourself the biggest, gaudiest diamond that I can find."

"Oh, no," she cautioned, and leaned her head beneath his chin as he carried her into the house.

"Gaudy isn't ladylike. Something significant . . . but tasteful . . . I think."

Case grinned. He was going to love being married to this lady. His L.A. woman.

ELEVEN

"Did you get all the leaves out of my hair?"

Lily's voice was muffled as she pulled the pink knit shirt over her head.

"Yes, darlin'," Case answered, as he dropped his boots.

"Are there any grass stains on my backside?" she continued, as she unzipped her pants and tried to swivel her head around to check.

"Yes, darlin'," he said, as his pants and shirt landed on top of the boots.

"I hope I didn't tear anything," she muttered. "I liked these pants."

"I do, too, darlin'. But I like them off better than I like them on."

The look in his eyes sent her knees shaking.

"Can you help me unhook my bra? My left arm is a bit stiff."

"Yes, darlin'," he drawled, "and that's because it's the one you were choking him with."

Lily blushed and stepped out of her panties.

Case plastered himself with a look of pure innocence as the last of his clothing fell on top of her own.

"Want me to scrub your back?"

She glared, suddenly aware that she was being mocked, and stomped into her bathroom and turned on the shower.

His arms were quickly around her, his chest at her back, as he turned her around and walked them both into the full force of the spray. His hands splayed out across her breasts, letting the water run between his fingers and down across her swelling nubs as his body betrayed his desires.

Lily moaned. She leaned her head back against his chest and let the water pepper down upon them.

"If I live to be a hundred, Lily Catherine, I'll never love you as much as I did today. You fought for me, and you fought for yourself."

"I did, didn't I," she muttered.

"You sure did, baby," he whispered. "Felt good, didn't it?"

"Not nearly as good as what you're doing now, Case."

His body was moving against her hips as his hands slid down across her belly and into her . . .

"Oh my God!"

The cry escaped, but Lily did not.

Case turned her in his arms and sent her backwards and down.

Tile at her back. Water on her face. Case inside her body. World upside down.

"There's something I have to tell you," Lily whispered, as their world came back into focus. She took the towel Case handed her and buried her face in its fluffy folds, muffling the words as she spoke.

"What the hell did you say?" Case yanked the towel away from her face and pinned her with blue fire. He couldn't believe what he thought he'd heard.

Lily sighed. She'd been afraid he'd take it this way. It was what had made her hesitate to call in the first place.

"I said: I talked to a doctor the other day. He says my face is healed enough to try some cosmetic surgery."

"I don't want you hurt anymore, Lily Catherine." Case's voice was agonizingly soft. "I don't want you to have to deal with the disappointment if it doesn't work. You're beautiful now."

"I know you love me as I am. That's why I can finally do this."

"I don't need this," he argued.

"No, I know you don't." Her touch was as gentle as her words as she laid her head against his chest. "But I do, Case. I do."

Case shuddered, emotions welling as he cradled her within his grasp. The thought of Lily in pain sent him to his knees

Lily gasped. She had no idea he would react this way. Her heart twisted at the torment on his face. She threaded her fingers through the wet tangles of his dark hair, and kneaded them on his shoulders.

"Darling, please get up."

But he refused. He closed his eyes. His whisper was so faint she almost didn't hear his plea.

"Lily, don't do this."

"Case! I don't understand? Surely you know I believe in your love? You know that I'll never leave you!''

"It isn't that," he whispered. "I don't want you to hurt just to be perfect for me. You're already perfect in my eyes."

"If I didn't believe that, I could never have made the call.''

Her voice was quiet, but it was the conviction with which she spoke that caught his attention. He was silent. For long agonizing moments neither spoke. And then Case's whisper nearly broke her heart.

"You'll marry me first. Do you hear me, girl? If you have to do this, you'll do it for yourself. Not for me!''

It was a promise she'd gladly keep.

"Do you have the ring? What happened to the ring? Who's got the flowers? Aren't we supposed to wear stuff in our buttonholes?''

J.D. and Dusty's coordinated chaos went in one ear and out the other as Case quietly tied his tie.

"You're gonna be wearing stuff elsewhere if you don't shut up," Cole grumbled.

"Cole!" Morgan Brownfield's admonishment did nothing to stem the confusion boiling in the back room of the tiny country church. "This is not the time to threaten your brothers," he muttered, although he felt the same way. The twins were driving everyone nuts.

Buddy sat calmly on a wooden bench against the wall and played the small, calculator-sized computer game that he'd brought with him from L.A. His suit was wrinkling, his shirt was on but buttoned one button off, and his tie hung limply around his neck, waiting for someone to come along and finish putting him together.

A tinny, computer version of a crowd roar echoed into the sudden silence of the room and Buddy jumped up from the bench with a look of glee on his face and yelled. "I did it! Hot damn, I killed the dragon! The princess is mine!"

Morgan rolled his eyes. "Do *not* curse in church."

Buddy looked up in amazement. He hadn't even realized that's where they were.

"Sorry!" he said.

Case grinned. Hell of a family he was getting.

"Everybody better be decent because I'm coming in."

The threat was not vacant as Debbie Randall pushed her way past Morgan and made a beeline for Buddy who was still enraptured by the fact that he'd just beat the computer.

"I won the princess," he crowed.

"That's nice, sweetheart," Debbie muttered, as she yanked him around and began unbuttoning his shirt.

"Lily said this would happen," she explained, as she smiled at Case. "She told me to come calm down the twins, put Buddy together and kiss her father."

Morgan leaned down for his kiss and smiled as she planted one swiftly on his cheek.

"Here," she said, as she took the computer from Buddy and stuffed it inside his jacket pocket. "Now for the tie."

He stood quietly as Debbie made him presentable. The twins had started to scatter the box of flowers a woman laid inside the door, when Debbie stopped them with a look.

"Wait a minute. I'll do it."

They complied without a word.

Cole watched in stunned silence. He'd never seen anyone quiet so many Brownfields with so few words.

"What did Lily say to do to me?" he asked gruffly.

"You don't want to know," Debbie drawled, and let her eyes roam across his tuxedo-clad shoulders as her hands could not.

Cole choked and turned several shades of red.

Case smiled to himself. He knew he'd been right. Cole was a goner. It was simply a matter of time before he realized it.

Debbie's small, curvaceous figure bounced from one man to the other, pinning boutonnicres, straightening ties, passing out combs for last minute hair grooming, until finally she'd done all she could to assure that her friend's wedding went as planned.

"Buddy," she said.

"Yes, ma'am," he muttered, suddenly overwhelmed by the fact that his sister was about to get married.

"Don't fidget, okay?"

He nodded. The computer game went off in his pocket and Debbie frowned. He handed it over without a word and watched wistfully as she dropped it into their suitcase.

"Twins."

They almost snapped to attention.

"You both look perfect. Don't redo anything."

"You got it," they echoed.

"Mr. Brownfield, you're about to get the best son-in-law a man could wish for. I should know. I've known Case all my life.''

Morgan nodded and smiled as Case hugged Debbie in thanks for all she'd done to assure there were no hitches.

Cole looked nervous. If there'd been anywhere to run he'd have taken it. He didn't know whether to be glad that Debbie was about to ignore him, or angry that he'd been singled out to be overlooked. He held his breath and then let it out in a slow, quiet whoosh as she walked toward the door. He'd escaped her fit of fixing.

He thought too soon.

''Got the ring?'' she asked quietly, as she sauntered by him.

Cole jerked. Surprised by the question. Nervous he could not supply the answer. His hand slid down into his pants pocket. He felt around in short, jerky movements, his heart thumping as he searched for the tiny circle of gold with which he'd been entrusted.

''Can't you find it?'' Debbie asked innocently.

Cole turned red . . . again. She wasn't talking about the ring, and they both knew it.

His hand closed on metal. Thank the good Lord!

''Yes,'' he snarled, as he pulled it up and held it in front of her face. ''I didn't lose a thing.''

Once again, it had been the wrong thing to say.

''Good. Never know when you might be needing that,'' she said cheekily, and left them in a huff of pink ruffles and lace.

''My dear, sweet Lord,'' Cole muttered, and leaned against the wall.

''Don't turn your back on that one,'' Case grinned.

*　　*　　*

"Something old, something new, something borrowed, something blue."

Lily's muttered reminder to herself ceased. The image of Case's eyes came instantly to mind. She'd never known anything bluer than his eyes. However, the thought did not help her predicament. She needed something blue.

A knock at the door sent her flying for cover. If she knew her man and she did, he wouldn't be waiting for her to come walking down the aisle. She was surprised he hadn't already made an attempt to see her.

"Who is it?" she called.

"Lily?"

"Case! Go away! You're not supposed to see me. It's bad luck!"

"Bull."

"Case Longren! The very idea. Cursing on our wedding day . . . and in church!"

"Are you decent?" he persisted. "Never mind. I'm coming in anyway."

"Case . . . no . . . wait . . . I don't . . ."

It was no use. He was in. He was staring. His belligerant expression disappeared. With glistening eyes, Case walked quietly toward Lily.

"You're so very, very beautiful, Lily Catherine."

Lily sighed. She walked into his arms and nestled her head beneath his chin, suddenly thankful she hadn't put on her veil. It felt awfully good right where she was. And there was always room for new traditions. This would be theirs. One last embrace before they said their vows.

Case stepped back, reluctantly releasing his hold

on his woman, and ran his fingers gently down the creamy lace covering her arms.

"My mother's dress," Lily said.

"My father's Bible." Case said, and handed her a small, worn, leather-bound book with the name *Charles Longren* stamped at the bottom in gold.

Tears shot to the surface and glittered, shining Lily's eyes to a tropical green.

"Darling, I don't know what to say, but I'm honored. It's perfect to carry."

Case shrugged. Lily could see he was moved yet unwilling to admit how deeply.

"I guess I'd better be going before Debbie comes sauntering through here and finds me."

Lily nodded her head and clutched the Bible tightly.

Case had started out the door when he turned, almost as an afterthought and muttered, "There's a flower pressed inside the Bible. It's from their wedding."

Lily's mouth trembled. She could tell this was difficult for him to admit.

"I'll be very careful with it," she said, and clasped it to her breast.

His last remark hung in the air between them as he walked out of the door. "It's a bluebonnet. My father was from Texas."

Something blue!

Lily started to shake. Suddenly she was alone. Beyond words at the *coincidence* that had sent Case to her just when she was searching for something blue, Lily opened the Bible.

It was brittle and yellowed, faded by the years. Yet it had outlasted the marriage, as well as the man who'd placed it so lovingly between the Words many years ago. The significance of its durability was not lost on her. She closed her eyes and prayed that they would be so fortunate.

Morgan Brownfield swallowed a huge lump in his throat and smiled back at the look of joy Lily was wearing. He allowed her to fuss as she straightened his tie, smoothed his hair across his forehead, and kissed him lightly on the chin.

"Love you, Daddy," she said gently.

"Love you, too, Lily Kate," he growled.

The music swelled. The small gathering of family and the assortment of friends turned in unison as father and daughter entered the sanctuary.

One collective sigh whispered through the audience at the look of radiance on Lily Brownfield's face. No one saw the scar across her cheek. They were too busy admiring the elegant young woman crowned in a halo of light from the single stained glass above her head.

Case caught his breath. *My Lily!*

He had to be the only man in the world who'd placed an ad for a cook and gotten an angel instead.

And then she was standing beside him, her hand resting in the trust of his own, as the minister's voice intoned the truth that was shining from Case Longren's eyes.

"Dearly Beloved . . ."

EPILOGUE

Lily squirmed. The chair by the window of her hospital room was not the most comfortable she'd ever occupied. But she knew it wasn't the seating accommodations that had her antsy. Today was the day the bandages came off of her face. Today she would be whole. Not some pieced replica of the real thing. Of that she was convinced.

Case stood against the wall and watched her impatience growing. He was scared to death. He didn't know what he'd do if she wasn't satisfied with the doctor's handiwork. A tiny voice kept niggling at the back of his mind, telling him that he might have to start all over with her if this failed. And then sanity would resume, and he knew that nothing would change between them. She was his life. And she'd allowed him to be hers.

"Lily?" Case watched her thoughts focusing.

"Hmmm?"

"We need to think about babies."

If he'd announced he was growing long ears and a tail, Lily could not have been more shocked. It wasn't that she was against the subject. It was just so far off the matter at hand that she was in a quandary.

"Think . . . or start?"

Case's expression was even more determined.

"I would like three. How about you?"

"I would like these bandages off my face first," Lily answered.

"Maybe next year, no later than the next. What do you think?" Case asked.

"I think you're not listening to me," Lily whispered.

She knew exactly what was at the bottom of his conversation. He was afraid she would leave. If her face was healed, he feared she wouldn't need him. If her face wasn't, he feared she would bolt.

"Case. I hear you. Do you hear me?"

He stalked across the room, gathered her in his arms, and buried his face in the silken swath of her hair.

"Well now! Are we ready to check the results?"

The doctor's question, as well as his presence, startled them. Neither was aware of his entry into the room.

"No! Yes!" echoed simultaneously with his question.

Case shrugged. His had been the dissenting vote. It didn't count. He stepped away and walked to the foot of Lily's bed as the doctor seated her on the side and began to remove the bandages, layer by layer.

Case wanted to look, but fear closed his eyes. Panic boiled in his gut and weakened his knees.

The doctor's exclamation of delight was obvious.

As was the cry of joy from Lily when he handed her the mirror.

"Oh! Oh my!" Lily whispered and ran a fingertip lightly across the pink but perfect cheek.

Only the faintest of traces remained and they would disappear within the coming weeks. It was as the doctor had predicted.

"Case! Look! Isn't it beautiful?"

Case opened his eyes. But he couldn't see through the tears. His voice was thick as he leaned against the foot of her bed and whispered.

"You always were, Lily Catherine. You always were."

SHARE THE FUN . . .
SHARE YOUR NEW-FOUND TREASURE!!

You don't want to let your new books out of your sight? That's okay. Your friends can get their own. Order below.

No. 101 HEARTSONG by Judi Lind
From the beginning, Matt knew Lainie wasn't a run-of-the-mill guest.

No. 102 SWEPT AWAY by Cay David
Sam was insufferable . . . and the most irresistible man Charlotte ever met.

No. 103 FOR THE THRILL by Janis Reams Hudson
Maggie hates cowboys, *all* cowboys! Alex has his work cut out for him.

No. 104 SWEET HARVEST by Lisa Ann Verge
Amanda never mixes business with pleasure but Garrick has other ideas.

No. 105 SARA'S FAMILY by Ann Justice
Harrison always gets his own way . . . until he meets stubborn Sara.

No. 106 TRAVELIN' MAN by Lois Faye Dyer
Josh needs a temporary bride. The ruse is over, can he let her go?

No. 107 STOLEN KISSES by Sally Falcon
In Jessie's search for Mr. Right, Trevor was definitely a wrong turn!

No. 108 IN YOUR DREAMS by Lynn Bulock
Meg's dreams become reality when Alex reappears in her peaceful life.
